JURASSIC UNDERWORLD

DANE HATCHELL

SEVEREDPRESS

JURASSIC UNDERWORLD

Copyright © 2024 Dane Hatchell

WWW.SEVEREDPRESS.COM

ISBN: 978-1-923165-37-3

PROLOGUE

"What do you mean the Earth is hollow and is alive with dinosaurs?" Erik Lott asked. The weathered Cajun brought down his glass of Laphroaig Scotch whiskey before it touched his lips. He adjusted his seat in the vinyl chair and straightened his back.

General Mitchell sat behind a dark pine desk with his hands folded on top of each other. "You heard right. The Earth is hollow, full of every dinosaur you can imagine. Every single bone you've ever dug up in your illustrious career is walking around down there with skin and muscle."

"And feathers," Lott said as he nervously fingered the black scarab charm held by a leather choker around his neck. He inhaled the warm campfire aroma from the Scotch and drained half the glass. "I have a background in archeology and paleontology. Discovered many antiquities from history—even secret Nazi treasures. I own a hunting and fishing guide service, but I've never been part of a rescue mission. Is there some information that you are withholding from me? A particular story, perhaps? Concerning Admiral Byrd in Nineteen Forty-Seven?"

"You mean the UFOs and Nazis he allegedly encountered in the hollow Earth?" Mitchell asked.

Lott's eyes widened. "You know the story. Are you telling me it was true?"

"I have no evidence that his encounters in the hollow Earth were true. From what we know, the Underworld is nothing like the one described in his diary. And I doubt the diary was genuine to begin with."

"It still begs the question. Why me? I haven't been on active duty for two years." Lott finished his drink and grabbed the bottle from the desk. He pulled the cork and glugged a pour into his glass—spilling some on the table before replacing the cork.

"A man with your credentials is unique in the armed services. You were a commissioned soldier for decades. Working at times with foreign governments while in the public sector—and them unaware of your connection to the military. The main reason we chose you was your level of security clearance. Few have attained your stature. This mission is so secret even the President has not been told," Mitchell said.

"This is a rescue mission," Lott said. "How do we get to the hollow Earth—or Underworld, as you have called it? An advanced tunneling machine using lasers or anti-matter?"

"There will be no 'we.' You are going alone."

"*Mais non*! I am not a one-man army." Lott downed the Scotch and then wiped his mouth with his fingers.

"You'll get there in a blended wing body aircraft equipped with conventional and unconventional engines. Onboard A-I will pilot the craft," Mitchell said.

"So, I fly over the North Pole and find an opening to this hidden Shangri-La? Like in Admiral Byrd's diary?"

"Not exactly." Mitchell reached for the bottle of Scotch and poured himself a drink. He lifted his glass toward Lott and took a sip. After grimacing, he said, "I don't know how you can drink that stuff. Tastes like I stuck my tongue into a pile of burned-up leaves." After a deep breath, he said, "Six months ago, the Russians were experimenting with Element One-Fifteen, also known as Moscovium. That element can only exist for milliseconds in certain conditions in the lab before decaying. An accident happened while trying to create a stable isotope of the element. The explosion wiped out an area half a mile around. Everything, and I mean everything around it, vaporized. The only thing left was a new stabilized isotope of Element One-Fifteen, smaller than the size of your fist. All the key scientists involved lost their lives. No one knows what caused the mishap or precisely how the scientists created the isotope. Putin was so cautious about the material that he had it shipped to a remote island until he could assemble a team to investigate what had happened. Some reports published by Russian scientists before everything was destroyed suggest that it may possess the power to warp space and time, according to our scientists here."

"It's theorized warping space and time would require incredible amounts of energy—something not much less than the energy produced in the Big Bang. If the Russians have discovered a power source capable of accomplishing that, we're in a lot of trouble," Lott said. "The Russians would take over the world and potentially the galaxy."

"Let's not get ahead of ourselves," Mitchell said. "The element opened a portal to the Underworld as the Ops team flew over the North Pole. We can pinpoint a physical location to which they transported, but it is unclear if the realm is in our dimension."

"If the Underworld is in a different dimension, how can you communicate with the Ops team?"

"We communicate with them using the new quantum entanglement equipment. The team of five is alive and well, but there's more to the story."

Lott picked up the bottle of Scotch and pulled the cork. "Let's hear it."

"Russian soldiers in pursuit of the stolen element crash-landed not far from our team," Mitchell said. "At this time, we don't know if any survived, but we must assume at least some did. Also, there's…"

The anthropologist raised the bottle and tilted the neck toward his glass. "There's what?"

"Neanderthals."

Before a drop of whiskey hit the glass, Lott brought the bottle to his lips and drank.

CHAPTER 1

A United States Intruder glided above the cold, turbulent waters of the East Siberian Sea. The Vertical-Take-Off-and-Landing blended-wing body, made of the latest stealth material, carried a Special Operations team of five on a covert mission. Three jet engines powered lift fans and provided forward thrust for an aircraft designed in the mysterious Area 51.

"How much longer?" Lieutenant Commander Jared Belazaire asked.

"Five minutes less than the last time you asked," Petty Officer 1st Class Markus Daniel said while navigating, his eyes glued to the low-level radar. The cockpit surrounding him was an array of transparent screens with multicolored indicators and digital switches with which to pilot. Graduating in Communications, he had the soothing voice of a late-night FM radio announcer.

Jared closed his eyes and shook his head. "Markus, you're a regular Dave Chapel." He raised his right hand and pointed. "Top of his class and a certified smart-ass." His face brightened. "Hey, that rhymes!"

Michael 'Gear' Babin, Petty Officer 1st Class, pulled his attention from the diagnostic routine on his electronic pad and said, "Yeah. You're a regular poet like Longfellow." The routine was completed and showed no errors, so he focused on the fuel supply. The tall man of Mexican heritage owed his citizenship to his grandfather, who served in World War II. Both his grandfather and father gave their all in military service. Though dying for one's country carried the greatest of honor, he had stayed alive to this point by delivering such honor to the enemy.

"Longfellow?" Jared repeated. "Let's keep my God-given gifts off the mission records." At five-foot-six, the thirty-year-old's ego elevated him to nearly ten feet tall. Growing up near the shores of the Mississippi taught him to survive on the bounty of the land. His mother ensured education came before any other distractions in the backwoods town. Jared graduated top of his class in college and the Naval Academy. The black man knew no limitations.

"We're flying pretty close to the water. What happens if one of those hundred-foot waves pops up from out of nowhere?" Sam 'Gym Rat' Micheli, Petty Officer 1st Class, asked. "Something that big could whack us out of the air like a flyswatter." The muscleman was the oldest looking of the bunch, even though all were nearly the same age. Excessive tattoos had that effect. Sam started training to fight MMA in his teens. His dedication led him to beat his shins daily with a broomstick to kill the nerves to reduce pain incurred during a match. He chose the military to give him an edge to become an undefeatable warrior.

"Believe it or not, I considered the possibility of giant waves," Bret 'Hammer' Handcock, Special Warfare Operator Petty Officer 1st Class, said. His red hair and freckles gave him a perpetual boyish appearance. "Wind generates most rogue waves. Top winds for the Anzhu Islands today are around twenty-three kilometers an hour. So, it's not enough to worry about waves hitting us at this low altitude. You should be more concerned if this area undergoes an earthquake." He had dreamed of racing cars when he was a kid. But his love of fireworks gave way to becoming a pyrotechnician while still in High School. The military offered a better way to make things go boom.

Rat took a swig from a bottle containing his protein drink, his tan bicep bulging, and said, "Earthquake? In the ocean? Who cares?"

"Tsunami," Jared said. "An earthquake in the ocean can create a tsunami—a big-ass wave."

"I thought a tsunami was like a hurricane. Except in the Pacific Ocean," Rat said.

Jared chuckled. "That's called a typhoon."

Rat closed his left eye and said, "I thought a typhoon was a—"

"Stop!" Jared said, with palms upturned. "Stop right there. Don't go digging the hole any further. Let's agree that you need to spend a little more time reading books than working out in the gym."

"But—"

"That's an order, Rat," Jared said. "I'm just trying to preserve your dignity."

There was silence before a deafening bout of uproarious laughter from the men save one.

"Bastards," Rat said under his breath.

"All right, gentlemen. The Anzhu Islands are ten clicks away," Markus said. "Shifting into ultra stealth...now."

The Intruder slowed, and the jet engines' slight hum disappeared.

"Engaging MetaMaterials," Markus said. "Okay, we're mirroring the surroundings. Invisibility, on!"

"This is spooky," Rat said through the eerie silence. "I don't like it."

"*Si*," Gear said. "I like the purr of an eight-cylinder HEMI more myself."

"You could hear a mouse fart," Jared said. "It'll probably be twenty years before this Skunkworks technology comes to light."

"This technology is a mercury plasma field propulsion engine," Gear said, crossing his arms. "The effect produces anti-gravity. It takes the place of the jet engines turning the fans when we switch to silent running. That story we were told about the silent running mode being an advanced form of noise cancellation is just a ruse."

"A mercury plasma field propulsion engine," Jared said. "How do you know that? Command gives us equal training. I realized everything about the mission was secret. This plane—us. We don't even exist. We're completely off the books. Information that sensitive would be above our paygrade, though—unless your Mexican heritage gives you special privileges."

"I got your special privilege right here," Gear said and pulled at his pants between his thighs. "I found the information on the internet after Googling it," Gear said.

"Say, what?" Jared asked.

"It wasn't that complicated. I was checking the material data safety sheets before the mission and discovered that this craft has a large quantity of mercury onboard. I Googled *mercury as a power source* and learned that spinning mercury at the right pressure and temperature can produce anti-gravity.

The T-R-B-Three and B-Two Stealth bombers reportedly have such an alternative power source available," Gear said. "The bubble under this jet is more than just radar and cameras. It also houses the mercury plasma engine."

"Hmm. The more you know," Jared said with words trailing.

"Rendezvous point in three minutes," Markus said.

"All right, you bunch of filthy animals. It's time to arm up," Hammer said.

Four men went to their respective duffle bags and lockers and began pulling out the unique weapons for their warfare.

"It's gonna feel strange going in with no bullets," Rat said as he buckled his tactical belt. "This pistol is nothing but a glorified paintball gun." He strapped a holster housing the weapon to his right thigh and adjusted the tightness.

"Yeah. This is some double-oh-seven stuff," Jared said while adjusting his knee pads. "I guess that makes Hammer like the 'Q' of this bunch."

"Who the frag is double-oh-seven? And what does 'Q' stand for?" Rat asked.

"Bond. James Bond. He had a license to kill. I kinda like that," Gear said as he straightened his cuffs before putting on his heavy jacket. "'Q' was his special warfare operator of sorts." Two green-colored vomit bomb grenades and two red-colored Jackass grenades went on his belt.

"For this mission," Jared started, "we don't have a license to kill. Don't want to be starting World War Three." He zipped up his jacket and picked up his full-head tactical helmet. The custom-fit headgear resembled a combination of a motorcycle helmet and a hockey mask. "I hate wearing this thing." After securing the apparatus, he said, "I feel like Darth Vader."

"What?" Rat said as he put the crown of his head in the helmet.

Jared slid his thumb on the right side of his mask. "Radio check."

"I got you," Gear said as he adjusted his helmet.

"I said, *I feel like Darth Vader*," Jared said. "Luke, I am your father."

"Darth Vader never said, *Luke, I am your father*," Gear said.

"He most certainly did, mister know-it-all," Jared said.

"That scene from Star Wars has one of the most misquoted lines ever," Gear said. "What Darth Vader actually said was, *No, I am your father*."

"Potato, po-tot-oe," Jared said.

"Hang onto something," Markus said. "I'm going to set this bird down."

The Intruder slowed to a stop, dropped the landing gear, and gently rested on solid ground. Markus looked up from his control screens and said, "All right. We're behind a sea stack of rocks for cover. The lab is only a football field away. It's two A-M, G-M-T plus nine hours. This time of year, it's night twenty-four seven. Nine degrees 'F'. There's no way of knowing the Russians' sleep schedule."

"Intel has it that there are only ten to twelve soldiers based on satellite recon," Hammer said. "I've got the Burner." He lifted the laser rifle across his chest. "Rat, you get to carry the load. Keep your peashooters by your side, and don't shoot unless you are sure you can hit your target."

Rat picked up a bag containing the bismuth container and hung it around his neck. The long strap brought the bag near his groin. "That's right. Load the mule."

"Are you ready?" Jared said. "Let's put on our Harry Potter cloaks of invisibility and get to work!"

"I hate it when you call them that," Hammer said as he lifted his gaze upward.

Each man gave an upturned thumb of approval and snapped the light-bending garment under their helmets.

A door opened at the craft's rear and descended to the ground. The five-foot steps offered just enough room for the soldiers to enter and exit.

The mission had begun.

CHAPTER 2

Jared was the first to hit the ground. His viewscreen quickly provided him with a 360-degree check and detected no threats to delay him. Rat was on his heels, so he hurried across the rocky terrain—leader's lead. The rocks would have hidden the Intruder even without it being cloaked, which meant he had to find a passable path over the rocks and onto the mainland.

Using simple commands from the neuro-net implant in his brain, his viewscreen plotted a course to enable him to achieve his objective. The night vision made him feel like he was playing a video game. Except in this game, the cold seeped through the layers of the cloak and jacket. He stepped up on a mostly flat rock and then found another foothold to elevate him to where he was waist-high to the ground.

The cloak covered his arms and hands, making maneuvering awkward. So, he laid his chest on the ground and rolled over until he could plant his feet. As he rose, the compound came into view. Just like the photos. Not much there. *The Russians must be terrified of this stuff to keep it way out here.* With a quick mental command, his viewscreen zoomed in on a small building and identified the thermal images of two people inside. Another area scan located a series of tripwires hooked to plastic explosives.

The other three joined him by his side.

"Two men on watch. Probably drunk on vodka by now," Jared said. "Be on the lookout for the tripwires. Your viewscreen should flag them."

"The other building. On the right. I get four signatures," Hammer said.

"Only six soldiers?" Rat asked. "On this whole island?"

"Unless there are people inside that cargo container guarding the element," Gear said. "But there aren't any ventilation ducts, so I doubt that's probable."

"That container is as cold as a witch's tit in a brass bra," Jared said. "Ain't nobody in there. This is going to be a walk in the park."

"Keep sharp, guys," Hammer said. "Let's not call victory until we're back on the Intruder with the mission completed."

"Let's head out," Jared said. "Single file." He felt the crunch of ice and whatever passed for grass with each step he took on this god-forsaken island. He carefully lifted his cloak and gently stepped over the tripwires to avoid eating steel pellets. But as his impish nature got the best of him, he hummed for the rest of the crew to hear. "De dum de dum de dum-dum, de dum de dum de dum-dum, de dum de dum dum dum."

After the third stanza, Gear said, "Jared, what's with the tune? This is the most sensitive mission we've been on, and you're acting the fool."

"It's the Enzyte commercial song. You know, the commercial with the goofy white guy with a big smile. He's happy because he takes Enzyte, and he's happy because life is bigger and better. I always hum that to myself because I naturally am *bigger and better* than most."

"Please, Jared, please," Gear said. "Don't you know where Enzyte got their tune from?"

"How would I know? Some songwriter made it up."

"No, genius. It came from the movie The Wizard of Oz," Gear said. "The tune is from the Scarecrow's song, "If I Only Had a Brain!""

"Wait, what? Oh yeah. I never put those two songs together," Jared said. "Never mind! I'm over it." He maintained silence until they were some twenty feet from the guardhouse. The small building had a frosted window that showed two soldiers sitting behind a long, narrow table. One soldier looked awake. The only entry point was a door in the back.

"Gear, you and Hammer take these two out," Jared said. "Rat and I will go to the other building where those guys are asleep."

"*Si, Jefe*," Gear said with feigned respect.

The two ghosts plodded in synchronization to prevent a glitch in the MetaMaterials from tipping the lone awake

Russian off. As they reached the door, they shed the cloaks and pulled out their side arms.

Hammer raised his right hand and threw up three fingers. Then two. Then one.

Gear opened the door, and Hammer was the first to enter.

The Russian looked up from his seat with glassy, fishlike eyes. When the pellet from the pistol hit his neck, his mouth flew open and froze. Then he slumped to the ground.

Gear placed the barrel of his pistol on the other's neck and pulled the trigger. "That's gonna leave a mark."

"Shack secured," Hammer said over the radio.

"Get over here," Jared said. "I can't take all the credit for this mission."

Jared and Rat had shed their cloaks and waited by the rectangular building housing the sleeping soldiers. Doors on either end provided entry and exit. They were on the south side, and Jared motioned Gear and Hammer to go to the other side.

Once in position, Hammer said, "Let's go with the Jackass grenades. They'll be confused to the point where they won't be able to think."

"Eh, those things aren't one hundred percent effective. I like the vomit bombs, myself," Jared said.

Hammer hesitated and said, "I like to show the enemy...some respect when I think it's due. Puking is so...demeaning."

"Oh, we have a Ruskie sympathizer. Tell us more, comrade," Jared said.

"Hey, watch what you call me. It's just...this is just too easy," Hammer said.

"Why not both?" Gear said.

"Done," Jared said. "I'll throw the vomit bomb. Hammer, you toss the Jackass on my mark." Jared grabbed a green-colored grenade and pulled the pin.

"Ready and waiting," Hammer said.

"On my mark. And three. Two. One." Jared waited for Rat to open the door and threw the grenade into the barracks.

Gear had opened the door for Hammer, and the red grenade went in and bounced across the floor.

The vomit bomb emitted a sound wave designed to do just what its nickname said, while the Jackass grenade's sound wave brought confusion. Their helmets shielded the team with countering waves.

Pandemonium broke out in the barracks. Shrieks of surprise and uncontrollable retching let the team know the attack was effective.

Three Russians stumbled from the south door and immediately dropped to the ground as pellets from Jared and Rat's guns found their targets.

The only soldier from the north door ran straight into a pellet from Hammer's pistol smack dab on the forehead.

"That was as exciting as shooting fish in a barrel," Jared said. "We'll have to drag them back inside, so they don't freeze to death." He turned to Rat. "We, meaning you, Rat. Hammer and Gear, move to the cargo container, and open the door."

"Why me?" Rat asked.

"I want to keep those big ol' muscles in shape," Jared said. "You said it yourself, load the mule."

Jared turned and headed toward the container. The wind had kicked up a bit, reminding him how much he hated cold weather. By the time he reached the cargo container, Hammer had the laser rifle pointed at a crudely welded door some jackleg had added.

"Fire in the hole," Hammer said. The blue beam from his rifle focused on the hasp of a bulky padlock. In no time, the metal slowly vaporized until it cut all the way through.

Jared and Hammer moved to the left of the door hinges while Gear maneuvered over and removed the lock. Using the door as a shield, he slowly pulled it open.

"I didn't hear a boom," Jared said. "That's a good thing."

Hammer passed Gear on his way to the opening with the butt of the laser rifle on his shoulder and his finger a hair away from the trigger.

Jared watched Hammer's view in the corner of his viewscreen. The container was pitch black until the infrared kicked in and lit it up.

The only thing in the room was a small, round object resting in the middle of the floor. Jared passed Gear and followed Hammer inside.

"I guess this is what we came for," Jared said. "Where's the mule?"

"I'm by the door wiping puke off my jacket," Rat said.

"Bring your ass, and that bag, over here," Jared said.

Rat stepped into the container and removed the bag from around his neck. "I'm glad to get that thing off. It kept getting in the way." He removed a twelve-inch by twelve-inch metal box six inches tall from the bag and pulled off the top. Dropping to one knee, he reached his hand toward the object. "This thing's no bigger than a golf ball." His fingers slipped off the object as he tried to lift it.

"What?" Jared said.

"Uh, it's stuck," Rat said. With more determination, he solidified his grip and lifted the ball from the floor. Then, put it in the metal box. "Man, that thing is heavy."

"Let me give you a hand," Gear said. The two placed the box in the bag.

Gear took out his knife and cut the bag's strap in the middle. "Grab hold of one end. I have the other."

"Thanks, man," Rat said.

"If you two lovebirds are done, it's time to return to the Intruder," Jared said.

"Man, why are you always busting our balls?" Rat asked.

"Oh, I don't know," Jared said. "I guess it just helps me pass the time. One thing is for sure: you will respect my author-i-tah."

"*Si senor* Cartman," Gear said as the two stepped out of the container with the element in tow.

"Ha! You got that right," Rat said. "He's about the same size as Cartman, too."

"You people," Jared said and then sighed. "Let's get the fudge out of here." After a pause, he said, "Markus!"

"Yes, sir."

"We'll be there in fifteen. Warm up the MREs. I'm ready to eat."

CHAPTER 3

The interior of the Intruder was equivalent to a large living room. The cockpit, situated toward the nose, had seats for both the pilot and co-pilot. Duplicate controls were available in the unlikely event of equipment failure. Six seats were available for the other team members for takeoff and landing—or if things got rough. Headspace was eight feet high, and a rectangular workbench/table took up eighteen square feet on the right side of the wing's body.

"Everyone strapped in and ready to go?" Markus asked.

Most of the men responded with a yo. Gear stood alone with his *Si*.

Markus transitioned into his radio voice and used his opening line from his college radio program, "Black, by popular demand.

"Ladies and gentlemen, boys and squirrels, this is your captain speaking. Please remain seated as we lift off this ice cube and ascend to the heavens on high. Be aware that overhead luggage may shift, and the drink between your legs may wet your crotch when I kick the rear jets in without warning. As always, puke in a bag, not on your teammate, and no grab-assing. Thank you for choosing Markus Daniel Airlines."

The blended wing body slowly lifted from the shore and picked up speed. The angle shifted thirty degrees, and the rear jet engines warmed to life.

"I wish this thing had a Millennium Falcon mode," Markus said. He engaged the throttle, and the g-force slowly pushed him to the back of his seat.

Jared felt relieved to be up in the sky, heading toward home. Leading a mission was something he had never seen himself doing. He was the youngest of his team and the highest-ranked. His success came from his knack for learning quickly and performing his duties as if he had been doing them for years. On more than one occasion, he'd been called an old soul. It was his confidence in his abilities that pushed him over the top.

The what-ifs weighed on him now—as always when he decompressed. What if his cocky action approaching the base had distracted one of his team members enough to miss a tripwire? What if there had been more Russian soldiers—maybe hidden underground outside of their viewscreen range? What if this strange new element becomes unstable, turning the Intruder and the team into vapor before reaching Alaska?

"Ladies and gentlemen, we have reached the cruising altitude of forty thousand feet. You may remove your lap belts and move about the cabin. Today's menu includes gopher guts, possum jowls and grits, and my favorite, cricket and grasshopper burritos. All the items are served in a hermetically sealed pouch with an expiration date not exceeding ten years. As always, thank you for flying Markus Daniel Airlines. Underwear on this flight is optional."

"Man, what's up with you?" Jared said. "Can't we have a little professionalism from the pilot? You spoiled my appetite with all that nonsense."

"Pot, meet kettle," Markus shot back. He turned to face his commander while smiling slyly. "I learned from the best."

Jared went to protest, but his mouth froze open without a response.

The others in the team burst into a loud bout of uproarious laughter.

Lowering his head, Jared said, "I'm over it."

An annoying buzzer pulled Markus away and back to his duties. "Uh-oh." His hands became a blur as he pushed the button and switch overlays on the LCD screens. "Bandit—from the Russian mainland heading to the Anzhu Islands."

"A day late and a dollar short," Jared said.

"Can you identify the craft?" Hammer asked.

"I'm getting some info now. The A-I will…wait. I have it. Hmm," Markus said, bringing a finger under his chin.

"Hmmm, what?" Jared asked.

"There is no match for the signature of this aircraft in the Russian database. It resembles a Sikorsky Raider X. Lockheed Martin is the parent company. That's one of ours," Markus said.

"Ain't no whirly bird gonna catch us out here," Rat said. The muscleman had gone into his bag and pulled out a rubber ball that fit comfortably in his hand. He bounced and caught it a few times, then began to squeeze and release the ball in exercise.

"This isn't a conventional helicopter," Markus said. He picked up an electronic pad and punched the screen in several places. He turned it around for the others to see—an image of a futuristic helicopter displayed on the screen. "The vehicle has twin counter-rotating blades for lift. It also has a jet engine instead of a tail rotor, unlike our Raider X, which has a propeller." He placed a finger from his other hand on the 3-D image and manipulated the craft to emphasize his points. "It's bigger, too. Big enough to carry eight men. With the rear housing an extended fuel tank."

"I didn't think the Ruskies had helicopters that advanced," Hammer said.

"They don't," Gear said. "If it's similar to the Sikorsky, you can bet the Chinese built it. They're masters at stealing our technology."

"You mean masters of buying our politicians," Hammer said.

"That too," Gear said.

The control panel flashed a new alarm. Markus acknowledged and said, "The chopper isn't descending. In fact…it's flying over the islands now."

"So, what?" Rat said. He had the ball in his left hand now and continued to exercise. "We're all stealthy and stuff. Gear told me even satellites couldn't detect us."

"They're climbing to forty thousand feet," Markus said.

"I didn't think choppers could fly that high," Hammer said.

"The air gets a little thin," Gear said, "but it's possible. That machine might have advances that can compensate."

"Can we outrun them?" Jared asked.

After studying the radar, Markus turned and said, "It's gaining on us, and it knows we're here. I don't know how."

"Great," Jared said.

"I could max out the jets, and we'd make it to the rendezvous point in Alaska before they intercept us. But then it would blow our cover. We could have an international incident leading to World War Three," Markus said.

"Then plan 'B' it is," Jared said.

"Right, boss." Markus turned his attention back to the controls and plotted the alternate destination.

"No Alaska? Where are we going? I hope it's someplace warm. I hate the cold. Plus, my tan is fading," Rat said.

"Markus and I don't need a tan," Jared said. "I don't like the cold either, but unfortunately, we'll be heading to Greenland. Hopefully, they'll give up the chase long before we arrive."

"Greenland?" Rat said. "Greenland is in the North Atlantic. We're in the Pacific. We'll be flying across the United States to get there." He bounced and caught the ball a few times.

After a loud sigh, Jared said, "Let me see your ball."

Rat held his next bounce and then tossed the ball to his commander.

"Okay. The Earth is shaped like a ball," Jared said as he held it before him.

"It's actually kind of pear-shaped," Gear had interrupted.

"Potato, po-tot-oe. I'm trying to make a point," Jared said. "Now, you're right. We're in the Pacific, and Greenland is in the Atlantic." Jared had placed a finger on the left side of the ball and slid it across to the right side. "But since the Earth is BALL shaped," he narrowed his gaze and looked at Gear, "we can fly over the top." He moved his finger from one side of the ball and over the top to the other. "And be in Greenland in just a few hours."

"Huh. That's pretty neat," Rat said and caught the ball Jared had thrown back.

"Yes, so we will fly over the North Pole," Jared said with wonder and magic. "And you know who lives in the North Pole? Santa Claus. Rudolf. Mrs. Claus. And all the tiny little elves who cobble their little hearts out day and night for good little girls and boys. Have you been a good boy this year, Rat?"

Rat raised his eyebrows. "Man, get out of here! Find someone else to make fun of. Why don't you get a job with Santa—you're about the size of an elf."

"Guys! Knock it off. We have a problem," Gear said, his gaze glued to the floor.

"What?" Jared asked.

"The bag…it moved!" Gear said.

"Look!" Rat said and took a few steps back.

The bismuth case pushed against the bag toward the cockpit. It vibrated and traveled slowly and steadily.

"It's making humming noises," Hammer said.

"I can't hear it. But working around engines all my life has taken a toll on certain frequencies," Gear said.

"I hear it," Jared said.

"It's gonna blow up! I just know it," Rat said.

"Well, it hasn't blown up yet," Jared said. He stepped over and opened the bag, exposing the box, and removed the lid.

The golf ball-sized element gave off an eerie emerald green glow. A fog-like mist formed above it.

"Keep that thing away from the controls!" Markus yelled.

"Gear, give me a hand," Jared said as he reached for the box. He grabbed two sides and tried to lift it. "Ugh! This thing is heavy."

"Here," Gear said as he bent down. "Try tilting it on its side. We can get our fingers underneath."

The two combined enough strength to get a hand on the bottom and slowly lift it.

"Put it on the worktable," Jared said.

The two quickly stepped in rhythm and placed the box on the three-by-six-foot metal table.

Gear removed two spring clamps from a drawer and placed the jaws on the end of the table—as a block to prevent the box from falling off. "I hope this holds."

The four team members gathered at the table and watched silently as the green mist hovered a couple of feet above the element. Then, the mist started to rotate.

"We have more problems than that green thing," Markus said. "We're being painted. The bandit is trying to lock its weapons on us."

"Is it that close already?" Jared said. "Can you push this wing harder?"

"Some, but then we won't have enough fuel to reach the new rendezvous point," Markus said.

"Where are we now?" Jared asked.

"Approaching the North Pole—about halfway from Greenland," Markus said.

The small spheroid's emerald glow intensified. Jared had to narrow his gaze because it was becoming painful to watch. Yet, he couldn't stop looking. An overwhelming force froze him in space, and time turned into something he could taste.

"What the hell!" Markus shouted. The aircraft shuddered.

"What's up?" Jared yelled. His words were colors leaving his mouth.

"On the radar! I…an anomaly. I don't know. There's a distortion—the camera shows what looks like a giant whirlpool made up of the aurora borealis. It's huge, and it's pulling us toward it! I've lost control!"

The control panel blasted an alert.

Markus silenced the alarm and shouted, "Incoming! The bandit launched a missile!"

Jared looked around the table. The other three team members stood watching the slowly growing spiral of green mist spin. Then, he could see through each of their eyes. His thoughts became their thoughts, and their thoughts became his.

The eerie, emerald glow became all he could see. It brought peace—tiredness as if resting after a hard day's work. He closed his eyes as his grandmother sang him to sleep.

Reality slapped Jared wide awake. Alarms screamed from the console in rapid fire. "Everyone, stay calm!" His training had kicked in. Even though he didn't know the situation, order had to be established. "Markus, report!"

"Radar's out. But…"

"But, what?" Jared asked.

"We're not at the North Pole anymore," Markus said.

"Then where are we?"

"Can't be sure. But there's a lot of green…trees and…I don't believe this," Markus said.

"Believe what?"

The aircraft's engines sputtered, and the winged body lurched before it lost altitude.

"Flame out! All engines!" Markus yelled. "Switching to stealth."

The wobbly craft steadied, and the gut-in-the-throat plunge smoothed to a stop.

The golf ball-sized Element 115 had returned to its dormant state. The green mist and all the other hallucinogenic effects were gone.

Jared felt the strength return to his knees and hobbled to the cockpit. "Talk to me, Markus."

Before the pilot could answer, the distinctive alarm of an incoming missile sounded its warning.

"Incoming! Countermeasures are kicking in!" Markus yelled. "It's close. Brace for impact!"

The explosion sounded muffled, and the aircraft responded like a car hitting a large pothole on the road. Jared expected a larger shoe to drop because life had taught him not to count his blessings too soon. For the moment, it seemed the worst was over.

"That was close," Gear said. He retrieved his electronic pad and started running diagnostics. "Jet engines are down."

"Where are we?" Rat said. He and Hammer had bellied up to the console to view the outside camera. "Wait! Look! There's—"

"Yeah. I see it, too," Hammer said. "But I'm not believing what I'm seeing."

There were a few times when Jared Belazaire was lost for words. Now was one of those times. "I see it… a dinosaur…where the heck are we?"

A massive beast with a long snake-like neck munched on the leaves of a tall tree. It looked bigger than four or five elephants placed end to end. The quadruped's tail was nearly as long as the neck, and it was dark tan with darker irregular stripes down its back and halfway down its body.

An alarm broke the spell of the strange world.

"We're losing altitude," Markus said.

"The silent running engine," Gear said. "It's losing efficiency. I guess the missile damaged the mercury plasma drive—it's probably leaking. Time to find a place to set this bird down."

"Scanning the area," Markus said. "Hang on…found something. I'll try to get us there in one piece."

The aircraft tilted at a twenty-degree angle. Team members standing grabbed for something bolted to the floor so as not to fall.

"How far?" Jared asked.

"Two miles. There's a clearing by a river. I got this," Markus said.

The Intruder glided through the air in a steady descent. True to his words, the pilot safely sat the blended wing body on the ground without a jolt.

"Nice flying," Hammer said.

"Yeah. But what do we do now?" Rat asked.

Four members of the team turned their attention to Gear.

"What? You expect me to fix this?" Gear said, his hands turned with palms to the sky.

"You are the mechanic," Jared said.

Gear's shoulders slumped. "I can't make chicken salad out of chicken shit."

"You better find a way to turn water into wine, or we're stuck here," Jared said.

"I've been looking over the data. We have fuel and pressure. We have fire. But we have no combustion," Gear said. "It doesn't make sense. Maybe if one engine was affected, not all three."

Jared started for the lockers on the left side of the wing. "Let's look outside. See if we can figure something out. Take the projectile guns. We're about to walk through Jurassic Park, and I don't want to be no dinosaur's snack."

At his locker, he retrieved his JNY-7 rifle. He pulled back on the charging handle and released, slapping the caseless .308 caliber cartridge into the firing position. A stable compound made up the bullet that exploded only on impact. "Grenade launcher firmly in place and three grenades in reserve. Side RPG, locked in. Full hundred round magazine." He pushed a button above the trigger mechanism, and a functional handgun detached. He checked the thirty-round magazine of 9mm exploding bullets, reinserted into the handgun, which he snapped back into the rifle. "Good to go."

The other team members quickly gathered their gear and prepared to leave the aircraft.

He turned his attention to Markus. "While we're gone, use the emergency communications. It's supposed to work even if we were on the other side of the universe."

"Yes, sir," Markus said and then followed protocol.

"Let's go with the standard helmet and E-goggles. The sensors show it's over ninety degrees out there."

"I was about to suggest that," Hammer said.

"I might get some tan time before we get out of here," Rat said.

"Let me lead," Gear said. "When you exit, get away from the aircraft. You don't want to inhale toxic fumes if the run silent engine is mercury plasma. Hit the ground and try not to breathe until you're well away."

"You heard the man," Jared said. "Let's go!"

CHAPTER 4

The exit door opened to the ground. Gear waited for the steps to unfold before taking them down. The air smelled hot and moist, scented with an earthy funk that reminded him of visiting a Panama rainforest. It filled his lungs, and when he exhaled, he felt a sudden surge of energy.

Once past the aircraft's shelter, he checked the area for threats. *Clear.* The river was two hundred feet or so away. Scrubby grass as tall as the top of his boot grew to the river and fifty yards on the other side of the aircraft, where a forest grew thick. No signs of life. *Good.*

The others piled out of the aircraft and headed toward him. Something about this place was unsettling. It was the light. Gear looked up at the sun, and his goggles dimmed the harmful brightness. It was high noon. Still, something felt off. There were no clouds in the sky, but there seemed to be a haze on high—unlike any weather conditions he'd ever seen.

"Anything catch your attention?" Jared asked. He was the last to arrive by Gear's side.

"All clear, so far," Gear said. "I haven't inspected the Intruder."

Gear stepped away from the team and increased his sight magnification to inspect the Intruder's belly. It was clean from that angle, so he picked up the pace to examine the other side. And it was as he suspected. A baseball-sized hole under the fuselage on the electronic housing meant the silent running engine was down for the count. Evidence showed that something hot, probably mercury plasma, escaped the hole. Closer inspection underneath showed it was free of any contamination on the ground. They didn't have to worry about hazardous materials. Whatever was in the plasma engine had puked itself over the pristine jungle before they landed. He went under the exhaust nozzle of the right wing and smelled the distinct odor of jet fuel. *That's not good.* He was just tall enough to reach up and run a finger along the outside of the exhaust nozzle. *Wet*. Gear inspected the other engines and found the same.

After joining the team, Gear said, "A missile fragment took out the silent running engine."

"But the cameras and other electronic instruments work," Jared said.

"I guess we got lucky," Gear said.

"I wouldn't call being stuck out here lucky," Rat said.

"What about the jet engines?" Jared asked.

"Well, I can tell you the fuel isn't firing in the engine. What I can't tell you is why," Gear said.

"Maybe whatever took out the silent running engine did the same to what ignites the fuel," Hammer said.

"I considered that," Gear said. "But it doesn't add up. The engines' igniters are on separate circuits from each other, with different power sources. The jet engines were designed to be as redundant as possible. If we lost one, we'd be fine with only having two. Under ideal conditions, we could make it with one engine for a short period. I found nothing wrong with the circuits when I ran my diagnostic. All three igniters and their spares can't fail simultaneously as they did. There's something about this place that's…different."

"I'll say. It has dinosaurs," Rat said.

"I feel it too," Hammer said. "That element, did it bring us back in time? Are we in a different dimension? Or a different world?"

"What if we are in the past on a different world in a different dimension," Rat said. "Maybe in the future, on a different world, in a different dimension. Or if—"

"OKAY," Jared said. "Come up for air, or you'll be like a dog chasing its tail."

"We don't have any answers for now," Gear said. "I suggest we head back to the Intruder and see if Markus made any progress. I'm getting a headache. We have enough nuclear battery power to keep the aircraft online for weeks. After that, I guess we'll have to find a cave."

"Caves have bats and spiders. We'll have to learn how to make bricks out of mud. Like in the old days," Jared said. "I'm feeling a little bad, too."

"Look! Over there!" Rat said, and pointed.

Up high, across the river, a twin-rotor helicopter fell from the sky.

"It's that Russian chopper. Its rotors are turning, but it's still falling," Rat said.

"That's called autorotation," Gear said. "Even though the engines are out, the blades spin because of the up-flow of air to help cushion the landing."

"Not from that high up," Hammer said. "No one could survive a fall that fast."

Two rows of rockets spitting blue flames from either side of the vehicle lit off. The boosters noticeably slowed the descent of the aviation marvel. The aircraft dropped behind the canopy of a thick forest.

A few minutes ticked by while the team looked on, and Jared said, "Well, that's not good."

"I didn't hear an explosion," Rat said.

"I don't see any smoke," Hammer said.

"We very well might have company," Gear said.

Black smoke rose from the tops of trees above the landing site. Then, orange and yellow flames licked up toward the sky. A muffled boom added a new chapter to the story of the downed Russian helicopter.

"Huh. I guess that means the landing was harder than we thought," Jared said. "Let's get back to the Intruder and see if Markus had any luck getting someone on the radio."

"Hey guys," Gear said. "How long do you think we've been out here?"

"Dunno," Jared said. "Twenty, maybe thirty minutes. Why?"

"The sun. It was straight up high noon," Gear said. "The sun hasn't moved, and the shadow from the Intruder hasn't shifted."

Jared looked at the ground, shook his head, and said, "Toto, I have a feeling we're not in Kansas anymore."

CHAPTER 5

Jared was the last one up the steps. Once aboard, he flipped the switch to close the door. He took off his goggles and walked over to his locker. "I need a shower." He removed his JNY-7 from his shoulder and hung it next to his helmet. "All of you need a shower."

"How about I hang up one of those scented Christmas trees like you have on your truck's rearview mirror?" Gear asked.

"Yeah, you can put that next to the fuzzy dice," Jared said. "Markus, report. Give me some good news."

The pilot chewed on dehydrated fruit from a brown package and raised his hand for pause. After swallowing, he said, "I do have good news. As you probably suspected, the terrestrial radio and satellite communications don't work. But I reached Command using the quantum communications."

"All right!" Rat said.

Markus took a sip from a can of water. "Command satellites followed us from when we left the Anzhu Islands until we reached the North Pole. Electronic countermeasures blinded the Russian and Chinese satellites capable of tracing us. They disrupted the communications of the Russian chopper as well."

"So, after reaching the North Pole," Hammer said, "where did we go?"

"Ladies and gentlemen, boys and squirrels, we are located over six thousand kilometers, over three thousand miles…inside the Earth," Markus said. "Try smoking that for a while."

"No way!" Rat said. He opened a can of water he had retrieved from the cooler and drank it. "We can't possibly be inside the Earth."

"Why?" Markus asked.

"Because of magma," Rat said.

Jared and Hammer locked gazes and then returned their attention to the pilot.

"You better not be pulling my leg," Jared said. "I like to cut up as much as you, but this situation is serious."

"Oh, ye of little faith," Markus said, raising his right hand and rubbing his eyes. "I don't play in situations like this."

"Go on, then," Hammer said. "I'm sure we have more questions than you have answers."

"Right," Markus said. "Command's A-I speculate that the Element One-Fifteen acted as a key to a *portal*, for lack of a better word, that placed us here. We don't know if we're physically inside the Earth or in some other realm of reality—maybe a different dimension. But at least we know we didn't travel back in time."

"Okay, can we get out of here?" Jared asked.

"There's a good chance," Markus said. "A tachyon scan from one satellite shows that the mysterious whirlpool that sucked us into it still exists above the North Pole. The Russian chopper went through it, too, later. Command believes a rescue unit can still enter through the whirlpool. The portal may stay open as long as we have the element down here."

"Or, it may not," Jared said. "Who knows? It might be gone in the next second. The sooner we get out of here, the better."

"Hold up, *amigo*," Gear said. "Our jets don't work down here. The Russians' jets didn't either. I need to do more research before we give them a go sign." Gear stepped over to a supply cabinet and pulled out an MRE. "Wait, let me try something." He opened the pouch and dumped it on the table near the element. After opening the accessory packet, he chose the book of safety matches. "This might support my theory." He struck a match against the striker, and it burst into a yellow-blue flame.

"Whoa! Look at that," Rat said. "It's brighter and burning faster than normal."

"Yep," Gear said. "I think there's more oxygen in this atmosphere than we're used to. I suspected that when I found raw fuel in the engine exhaust. When I took my first breath here, I immediately felt a boost in energy. After some time, I started to get a headache. I figure our bodies need to adjust to this new O-two level."

"Make yourself useful, Rat," Jared said. "Grab the gas test machine and get a reading."

The soldier downed his water, crushed the can, and disposed of it. He then retrieved the hand-held machine and powered it up. It made a series of beeps, and the pump's hum purred like a kitten. The beeping stopped, and the display lit up. Rat pushed a button two times and said, "Reading thirty-five percent. That's pretty high, right?"

"Indeed, it is," Gear said. "In prehistoric times, the O-two level was thirty-five percent, just like here."

"What does that mean for us?" Hammer asked.

"It means our jet engines can't run until we have the proper air-fuel mixture," Gear said. "I can't modify the engines without the right tools and equipment."

"And the silent running engine is toast," Hammer said.

"Markus, fire up the Twitter machine and call Command," Jared said.

"It's called 'X' now," Markus said.

"Potato, po-tot-oe," Jared said. "Tell them to call Area Fifty-One and send one of the anti-gravity planes that don't exist!"

CHAPTER 6

A massive emerald whirlpool spinning above the North Pole pulled the Chinese-made Z-25 helicopter into the void.

Pilot 1st Class Lieutenant Nikotay 'Kolya' Pavlov saw the world go black. The jet engine's roar and whine of the rotating blades stopped as if someone had flipped a switch. The silence had him wondering if he had died, and he expected his thoughts to stop abruptly. Instead, the gray skies and icy terrain underneath gave way to a soft blue horizon painted above lush green.

Kolya gripped the controls and gasped like he was coming up for air after a deep dive. The engines spat and sputtered, and his alarm panel lit up like a slot machine he once played at Altai Palace Casino.

"What's happening?" Captain Viktor Kuzmin shouted.

Gathering his bearings, Kolya said, "Engines are dead. Prepare for an emergency landing."

"Assume the crash position!" the captain ordered.

After several unnerving seconds of watching the trees underneath become more defined, a wave of relief washed over Kolya when the chemical rockets kicked in. The helicopter's descent slowed, and the machine bobbed in the air like a boat in rough waters.

Something caught Kolya's attention as he glanced up from the controls. In a thin patch of forest, a giant creature nearly as tall as the tree it stood next to looked in his direction and opened its mouth as if issuing a warning.

The world then turned on its side as the helicopter descended onto the sprawling canopy of the forest. The cockpit shifted at a ninety-degree angle, and the machine violently bucked as the blades chewed into foliage and wood. Metal groaned, limbs snapped, and men screamed. The harrowing moments had slowed time, but as the helicopter came to rest, it brought with it a reassuring calm.

I'm alive. Kolya turned in his seat to check on his comrades. It was difficult as the cockpit leaned on its side and was still in the clutches of thick tree branches. The tail boom tilted slightly toward the ground.

"Is everyone safe?" Kolya asked.

"We are secure," the captain said. "A few bumps and bruises. Nothing compared to what will happen if I find you caused us to crash."

"I smell fuel!" 3rd Lieutenant Mikhail 'Misha' Zaitsev said.

"We must evacuate before there is fire," the captain said.

Buckles clanked from release, and men fumbled about. Kolya positioned himself near the door and unlocked it. The angle was such that it required less effort to slide the door along the track. "We are about five meters from the ground. There are branches, so we do not have to jump."

Kolya was first out, grabbing onto a nearby branch. His weight lowered him enough to grab another branch. Which lowered him enough to let go and drop safely to the ground.

A hole in the fuel tank had the combustible running down the tail boom onto the ground.

"You must hurry," Kolya called out.

Second Lieutenant Dmitriy "Dima" Titov was next, followed by Misha, 2nd Lieutenant Ivan "Vanya" Orlov, and 3rd Lieutenant Aleksandr "Sasha" Sokolov. The only two remaining were the captain and Sergey Belov.

Next out of the plane were a mixed combination of VSS Vintorez "Thread Cutter" rifles, ammo cans, and duffle bags.

The men hurriedly removed the items from the ground and set them by a tree several meters away.

A sudden whoosh and fire blazed mightily from the hole down to the tail boom.

"Captain! Sergey! You must leave now. Fire! Fire!" Kolya screamed.

The trees cradling the metallic bird immediately ignited, sending smoke and a chorus of pops and roars as matter turned to energy.

Frantic, the men called out for their comrades to jump to safety.

A high-pitched whistle, sounding like a tea kettle ready to serve, set Kolya into survival mode. "Run! Run!" His mind went blank as he haphazardly sped through the forest. Roots and underbrush had him stumble but not fall several times.

And when the helicopter exploded, he ended up with his face planted in moist, rotting leaves.

The danger was behind him, and his military training had him back up on his feet and assessing the situation. Fire blazed in the short distance beyond the branches. The surviving teammates were all in sight and uninjured. *The guns.* "We must get our equipment!" Kolya led without waiting for acknowledgment.

The forest was ablaze, and flames neared the tree with the supplies. Kolya felt the heat as he approached the rifles. At first, it felt like a hot, breezeless afternoon. Then, it felt like the searing heat coming from an oven. His instincts warned him to stop, but he did not want to be in this unknown land with only his sidearm.

Kolya turned his back to the blaze to shield his face as he slung two rifles over his shoulder and picked up two ammo cans.

Dima and Vanya rushed past him as he fled into the forest, lugging his heavy burden. Sasha and Misha trailed.

What to do next? They were no longer in the icy cold of the north. No radio. The captain was dead—Sergey, too. Nothing could have survived that explosion. The speed and intensity with which the fuel burned amazed him.

Concerned he would lose his comrades, Kolya slowed his steady march and stopped. He lowered the ammo cans to the ground and felt his tight arm muscles relax.

Vanya stumbled near him with his arms wrapped around three rifles. Dima was right behind, with one rifle and two duffle bags. Sasha arrived with one duffle bag, and Misha was empty-handed.

"We must find safety," Kolya said. He gathered his senses momentarily and watched the foliage blowing in the wind. "Everyone take one rifle. We will leave the other behind.

"Sasha and Misha, put the ammo cans in each bag and carry them, too. I will take the other bag." He paused long enough for the men to follow orders. "We will go this way—upwind to escape the fire." He didn't wait for a consensus and led the way.

Minutes ticked by. The muggy heat quickly dripped sweat down his face, into his eyes, and down his back. Along with his discomfort, sounds in the forest had his head jutting from side to side. The origin might have been from small animals or birds. With all the dried foliage, he feared a poisonous snake might strike at every step.

Then he heard something rustling louder nearby. He raised a fist, slowed to a stop, and brought a finger to his lips. The rustling continued, and it was close.

An unusual animal sound from a few meters away had the team freeze and turn their eyes toward it.

Kolya thought it resembled a combination of a crow's call and snake-like hiss.

Then, the creature shrieked—raising the hair on the back of Kolya's neck. He dropped the duffle bag and pulled the rifle off his shoulder, readying it in the firing position.

The other soldiers prepared for combat.

Something in the distance moved to Kolya's right. He spun quickly but couldn't see beyond the trees.

More shrieks had the soldiers sweeping the rifle barrels side to side, with fingers millimeters away from the triggers.

A strange creature scurried from the cover of one tree to another. It uttered a slow, repeating rasp. A brown feathered crest on its crown matched the feathers on its short, skinny wings. Kolya found it to be about the size of a large goose. The bird-like features mixed oddly with those of a two-legged reptile.

Curiosity or bravery had the Velociraptor step into view. Its head hung low as it moved from side to side. Then it rose high and back, with the mouth opening to show saw blade-type teeth.

"What is it?" Dima asked. The large man's nose was misshapen—a casualty of years in the boxing ring.

"It looks like a creature from the prehistoric past," Sasha said. The fascination had his eyes wide on his thin, sharp face.

"You have been watching too many movies," Vanya said, the oldest on the team who had seen more combat than the others combined. "Kill it and be done."

"I give the orders here," Kolya said. "The captain is gone. I am the highest-ranking officer."

"We are wasting time," Vanya said.

"What difference does it make?" Misha asked. "We do not know where we are going. We don't even know where we are." East Asian ancestry distinguished him from the Slavic features of the others.

The Velociraptor jutted its head forward and shrieked as it charged for attack.

Kolya had let his guard down and cursed himself for his incompetence. A haphazardly fired shot missed the target, and the demon bird closed the distance between them.

More cries from nearby predators meant the dire situation just increased exponentially.

Vanya's rifle spat a 9x39mm bullet from the Vintorez's suppressed barrel. It hit the Velociraptor mid-stride and sent it reeling sideways. The blue-tip, armor-piercing round was overkill.

Sasha cried out in blood-curdling pain.

The soldier lay face down with the Velociraptor's claws dug into his left thigh and the creature's evil mouth tearing at the shirt on his back.

"Sasha!" Kolya yelled.

"There are more," Vanya said, who raised his rifle and sighted a target.

Kolya saw more creatures leave the trees' concealment and head straight for the group. Dima had lifted his rifle to shoot Sasha's attacker. The Velociraptor held on tightly as his prey rolled over and over on the ground, trying to escape. "Do not shoot!" Kolya said. "You will hit Sasha. I will help him."

By this time, Misha had joined Vanya in firing at the oncoming dino-birds.

One Velociraptor missed Vanya's latest shot and was less than a meter away from him when the soldier took the butt of the rifle and knocked it in the head—rolling it to the ground. The soldier quickly squeezed the trigger, eliminating the threat.

Tossing his rifle, Kolya reached for his ballistic knife on his hip and jerked off the protective sheath. His comrades continued to fire, but he had to trust them without his lead. "Hold still," he yelled above Sasha's cries of agony. He dropped to one knee by his comrade's side and plunged the blade into the back of the Velociraptor.

The dinosaur shrieked but did not let go of the tender flesh it greedily tore from the human's back.

Determined to win at all costs, Kolya jabbed the knife again and again until one of the Velociraptor's claws was released from the thigh and onto his left forearm. The black talons dug deep as blood gushed out.

The pain made him sick to his stomach, and he gagged. But he could not let the evil monster win. In mad desperation, he put the blade under the dinosaur's long neck and sawed back and forth. Blood gushed over his hand, but in seconds, he felt the creature's spine give way to steel. The blade, no longer facing resistance, came back toward him, and the tip slightly penetrated his chest.

Kolya pulled the deadly talons from his arm, turned, and sat on the ground, trying to regain his bearings. An instant later, he heard Misha scream out his name. His eyes fixed on another Velociraptor almost upon him. Without a second to lose, not even taking a moment to breathe, the pilot pulled the pin on the spring-loaded knife and pointed the blade at his attacker less than a meter away. He pushed a lever on the handle, releasing the spring, and shot the blade with enough force to penetrate protective armor.

The dying caw of the Velociraptor told him he had killed his adversary. Kolya gazed up to see his comrades staring at poor Sasha.

"Nice shot," Vanya said to him. "Not so nice for our comrade."

"Is…" Misha's voice had cracked. "Is he dead?" A tear rolled down his left cheek.

"In shock or dead," Kolya said as if to himself. He reached for the man's wrist with his right hand, but pain and dripping blood from his left forearm forced him to pull back.

"Wait," Misha said. "I will get the medical kit." The young soldier headed toward one of the duffle bags.

Dima lowered to one knee and placed a finger at the base of Sasha's neck. He repositioned his hand a few times—trying to find a pulse, but gave up with a quick shake of the head. "He is beyond our help. May the earth be soft for him."

"Stay alert," Kolya said. "Other dangers may await us." Staying there too long was not a good idea. The dead creatures were sure to lure scavengers into the area. Moving the fingers on his left hand became difficult.

"How bad is it? Do you have any broken bones?" Misha asked. He knelt by Kolya and opened the medical kit.

"I do not believe any bones are broken," Kolya said. "Stop the bleeding as fast as you can. We must leave as soon as possible—"

Kolya gasped and grimaced as cool liquid splashed on his wounds and then turned into fire.

"I am sorry. This will kill the germs," Misha said. The soldier hurriedly cleaned the wound and applied a medicinal ointment before wrapping the forearm with gauze. "I want you to take this antibiotic." He handed the leader a pill and a canteen.

The water hitting his mouth made Kolya realize his thirst. He was ready to chug more down but came to his senses. There was no way to know how difficult it would be to resupply water. Even after all the training and missions he'd been on, this was the most uncertain he'd ever been. But he was in command now. His comrades depended on him.

Feeling a hostile presence, Kolya turned his eyes upward and saw Vanya's critical gaze peering down.

"Orders?" Vanya said with impatience.

The commander placed his weight on his right hand and stood. "We are deep in a forest somewhere. Our best path forward is to find a clearing…and then a high point to get a better view. Perhaps find a village and a way to reach home. Our supplies are only good for a few days. We must complete our mission and report. As we have found, this place has unexpected dangers. But without risks, we will not drink champagne," Kolya said.

CHAPTER 7

"Command says it's going to be thirty-six to forty-eight hours before a rescue craft can attempt to reach us," Jared said. He had just finished a delicious MRE of chili and beans. "I don't plan on staying inside this tin can with the rest of you the whole time. Especially after eating those beans. We're in a strange place, and I'm curious to see what we can find."

"I'm up with that," Rat said. He held his rubber ball in his right hand and flipped it up. It dropped and landed on his bicep, bouncing back up and into his hand.

"There's still a possibility that some or all the Russians made it out of the helicopter before it exploded," Hammer said. "I believe we have the advantage of at least knowing what direction they could come from. I doubt they had time to get a fix on us before going down."

"Perimeter radar reaches almost as far as the river," Markus said. "Nothing can sneak up on us."

"Okay, well, we're trained military, so we know how to watch our backs in unfamiliar territory," Jared said. "And I don't plan on searching for any Russians. That's like looking for trouble. We have a plan, and all we have to do is stick to it. After a couple of days in the woods, we'll be back in the air and on the way home. I'll be waving bye-bye to those commie bastards, saying '*Adios*, mother-fuckers.'"

"What about that big ugly dinosaur, like we saw before we crashed?" Markus asked. "If there's one, that means there're more."

"That dino was bigger than an eighteen-wheeler," Hammer said. "It was eating leaves, so I doubt it'd be interested in us."

"Correct, *amigo*," Gear said. "I believe what we saw was a Brachiosaurus. It was, or I guess what I should say is, a herbivore."

"Brachiosaurus?" Jared said. "I thought what we saw was a Brontosaurus. I've never heard of a Brachiosaurus."

"Think of a Brontosaurus more like an enormous elephant. Sure, it had a long neck, but its front and rear legs were closer to the same size. Whereas the Brachiosaurus had longer front legs, a longer neck, and stood as high as fifty feet compared to around thirty feet of the Bronto," Gear said.

"Thank you, Doctor Doolittle, for that valuable lesson," Jared said, letting his eyes dance upward.

"I don't know why I bother," Gear muttered.

"I'm going to get some sun," Rat said while shedding his shirt. He pulled the tee shirt off and tossed both on top of his duffle bag. The young man stretched his arms and raised his fists toward his ears. "Look at these guns." His biceps and deltoids flexed and bulged.

"The testosterone is getting thick in here. I'm going out too," Markus said.

"Someone has to stay in the Intruder," Jared said.

"I'll stay," Hammer said. "I'll work with the A-I and set up our defenses for maximum benefit."

"Bring your rifles," Jared said as he removed his shirt. "And your goggles. We can leave the helmets here."

CHAPTER 8

The four men exited the Intruder and scanned the area for threats. The sun was still beaming directly overhead, and there were no clouds to filter the harsh rays. *I was taught the inside of the Earth was a molten combination of metal and rocks*, Jared thought. *This place looks like it's out of the movie Jurassic Park*. Beads of sweat formed on his neck, and his armpits already felt wet. *We need a good breeze to kick up*.

"Hey, look over there," Gear said, pointing to the sky.

Above, two strange creatures soared. They had large, bat-like wings that were pointed at the end. A big triangular-shaped head jutted forward on a swan-like neck.

Jared zoomed in with his goggles and got a better look. The creatures had skinny bodies and claws at the ends of their arms. Another set of bigger claws on their feet trailed behind, almost looking like a tail. "That must be a bat's ugly cousin."

"It's a pterosaur," Gear said.

"I thought they were called Pterodactyls," Jared said.

"A Pterodactyl is a pterosaur. Pterosaurs are flying reptiles," Gear said.

"I thought a Pterodactyl was a flying dinosaur," Rat said, sweat glistening off his naked chest.

"No, *amigo*," Gear said. "Scientists have divided dinosaurs into saurischians, which means lizard-hipped, and ornithischians, which means bird-hipped, based on the arrangement of their hip bones. What's flying up there is probably a Pteranodon. Pteranodons are larger than Pterodactyls."

"That head reminds me of Woody Woodpecker," Jared said.

"Let's go to the river," Markus said. "There might be fish. I could go for some fresh food. Those MREs must be fifty percent salt."

Jared pushed a switch on the right side of his goggles. "Radio check."

"Loud and clear, Captain," Hammer said.

"Watch your step, guys," Jared said. What was it about the sun? It was about the same size as the one topside, but there was no way it was a star. His sense of adventure gave way to fearing the unknown.

The ground felt hard and had sparse patches of grass. On the other side of the river, trees grew along the bank. Trees also grew on their side of the river, but not until several hundred feet in either direction. By the time they reached the river's edge, he saw why. The bank was solid rock.

"I was wondering why there weren't any trees in our area," Jared said. "It's all rock."

"Granite, from the looks of it," Gear said. "That means this area was under earth for an amount of time. And magma in the mantle crystallized under pressure—forming granite. If we are actually inside the Earth in our dimension, that suggests someone carved out where we are after the granite formed," Gear said.

"I was just about to say that," Jared said mock-matter-of-factly. "Anyway, I'm more interested in what's in the water." The river was about thirty feet wide and had a mild current. It was a strange greenish color that was still surprisingly clear. He adjusted the settings on his goggles and scanned closer to the surface. There was no way for him to tell how deep the river ran.

Markus had descended to a lower level and was much closer to the water. "Hey, I see fish… They're a good size. They remind me of choupique. Looks twice as big as the ones I've caught, though."

"Trash fish," Rat said. "Only good for bait."

"Not so fast," Jared said. "If you cook choupique soon after you catch them and take a little time preparing, you can fry the meat or make some potato patties with it."

Rat hopped down near the river next to Markus. Getting on his knees, he scooped a handful up, brought it to his nose, and sniffed it. "It smells okay—not too bad. There's a slight funk, but I've swum in worse water."

"I wonder if there are any catfish?" Markus asked. "I'd much rather eat that."

"Catfish have been around since prehistoric times," Gear said. "Only one way to find out. Drop a line and see."

"Wait, what's that?" Markus said.

"Where?" Rat said.

"Over there," Markus pointed to the other side of the river. "That silver pole sticking out on the bank."

"I see it, but I don't know what it is," Rat said. "Do you want to go check it out? It looks man-made."

"I have no intention of swimming these waters to check out a three-foot pole," Markus said.

The radio squawked over the channel, "Movement, ninety degrees left of the river." It was Hammer's voice.

Jared turned and saw several—maybe eight—human-sized, two-legged creatures. They were moving fast and heading straight for them. "Heads up! We got a lot of GEICO lizards coming from my left. Lock and load. I don't think they're selling insurance."

"Troodons!" Gear yelled.

Jared and Gear raised their JNY-7s and sighted the targets. Markus and Rat hurried back up the rocky bank to flat land.

The dinosaurs had reptilian-looking heads, long legs, and medium-sized feathered arms. They oddly reminded Jared of a combination of an ostrich and a two-legged lizard with short feathers on the body. "Man, they're moving fast." He picked the lead threat and squeezed off a round. The exploding bullet hit directly in the chest, almost blowing off the left wing.

The other Troodons sidestepped to avoid tripping on their companion but kept charge without slowing down. By this time, they were twenty yards away.

Gear and Jared fired in rapid succession, using the automatic aiming feature of the JNY-7.

Blood splatted and shot in the air like fireworks. Troodons scratched and screamed as each fell to the modern ordinance. Pieces and parts hand grenaded across the tan-colored ground. The attack was over well before becoming a real danger.

By the time Markus and Rat arrived, the incident was over.

"What, you didn't save me one?" Rat said, lifting his rifle to the fire position. "Those things look badass."

"The area is secure," Jared said over the radio.

"Ten-four," Hammer replied.

The team walked over to the kill to check out the prehistoric creatures.

The slender legs had raised sickle-shaped claws on the inside of the feet. Olive-green skin was underneath the short feathers on the body, and golden stripes marked its spine. The yellowish eyes had blade-like pupils looming over the beak with rows of sharp teeth.

"I don't think they taste like chicken," Jared said.

"I'm going to cut off a foot and bring it back. Hang it from my truck mirror as a conversational piece for my dates," Rat said.

"I'd think twice about doing that," Gear said. "You don't know what bacteria or pathogens it may carry. It could be the death of you out here."

"Yeah. Don't touch *dat,"* Jared said.

A thunderous roar emanated from the wooded area from the same direction the Troodons had come.

"What the hell was that?" Jared said.

"Dunno, but it sounded big," Markus said.

Tearing through the woods, a huge two-legged dinosaur ran, its massive head outstretched, and its mighty jaws unhinged. It uttered a high-pitched, agitated cry as thick legs carried it quickly toward them. The dinosaur had skin the color of an elephant and arms that looked comically short. A thick, short tail followed and swished side to side.

"That head makes almost a third of its size," Jared said.

The radio broke in, "Team, there is—"

"Yeah, Hammer, we see it," Jared said.

"I'm dialed in," Markus said. "Those teeth are as big as Bowie knives."

"Team, meet Tyrannosaurus rex," Gear said.

"Heck, even I know that," Rat said.

The dinosaur roared again, each foot balancing ten tons and pounding the earth.

"That beast is moving," Jared said. "Better stop it now—sight in on its chest. Rat, use your RPG. Get ready to fire on three." Jared swallowed and licked his lips. "One, two, three!"

The JNY-7s spoke in unison, mixed with the zip of the rocket-propelled grenade. The bullets exploded first with their distinctive pops, only to be drowned by the blast of the grenade.

Unstable, the behemoth's legs buckled as its torso nearly ripped in half its left side. It fell and slid on its belly, with its head cocked sideways, sending dust eddies to either side until it came to a grinding halt.

"Target down," Jared said over the radio. "Let's go take a look, guys."

Two threats in a short amount of time. And they were out in the open. There was no telling how many or what hid in the woods. Jared's sense of adventure had met its quota for today.

The smell of the T. rex hit them well before their arrival. It was as long as a school bus, measured from nose to tip of tail. Red blood-stained chunks of meat splattered over the body. The arms were short but had two four-inch claws on the end that looked like they could shred Kevlar.

"Look at the size of its feet and those big ugly Frito-colored toenails," Jared said. "They're almost as big as me."

"I'm surprised how the blood is so mammal-like," Markus said. "And the meat…reminds me of pork. Might barbeque up nicely."

"Your stomach always thinks out loud," Jared said. "You eat twice as much as I do and are skinnier than a beanpole."

"I like to try the indigenous dishes when I travel," Markus said. "When in Rome…"

"Well, at least we know why the Troodons ran out of the forest," Gear said. "I guess we were in the wrong place at the wrong time. The T. rex must have been on a hunt."

"Can we take the head with us?" Rat asked.

"Man, are you crazy?" Jared asked. "We ain't bringing that slimy, overgrown two-legged gator anywhere close to the Intruder. Probably couldn't get it up the ramp. And we ain't strapping it to the wing."

"Uh, guys," Markus said. "I don't think the T. rex was chasing the Troodons."

"What makes you say that?" Gear asked.

"Over there," he said and pointed toward the woods.

A mass of humans emerged between the trees in a line that stretched thirty yards across. They stepped slowly and steadily, and more followed those who led. Each held a primitive weapon and wore brief animal-skin clothing.

"There must be a hundred of them," Jared said.

"Team—" the radio started.

"Yes, we know," Jared said. He considered firing a warning shot, but the JNY-7's suppressed discharge wasn't likely to spook them away if the noise made by the RPG didn't.

"Captain?" Gear said. "Orders?"

Jared turned his gaze back toward the Intruder and considered running for it. He wasn't confident they could make it before being within range of the spears some of those cavemen carried or even being outrun. Any human surviving in an environment like this was bound to be in prime physical shape.

"I say we fire," Rat said. "Drop a few, and the rest will go to running."

"What about, you know, the Prime Directive?" Markus said.

"What you mean, Prime Directive?" Jared said. "This ain't Star Track. I ain't wearing a red shirt and be the first to die."

"Star Trek."

"Whatever."

"This is their world. We're the interlopers. What we do or do not do could influence their evolution," Markus said.

The cavemen moved as if all were part of a coordinated plan.

"And if they kill us, it will influence evolution in the world we came from," Jared said. "I still got babies to make."

"Neanderthals," Gear said. "Look at the head shape, the barrel chest, and the shorter forearms and legs below the knees."

"Neanderthals?" Jared said. "You mean like evolution and stuff? You might be a monkey's uncle, but I'm not. The Bible says God made Adam and Eve. They ain't nothing but a bunch of people living in caves that stunted their growth."

"There may be a way to reason with them," Gear said. "The difficult part will be the communication."

"Let's slowly back up," Jared said. "Put a little more space between us and see how they react. If they think we're weak and attack…light them up with all we have—grenades, RPGs, bullets. We'll hit them hard…try to disorient them. Then we'll head to the Intruder. Let's move."

The four men backed away, matching a step for every step forward by the lead cavemen. Fortunately, the retreat didn't incite an unfavorable response from the natives.

The cavemen reached the T. rex. A few lined up in front of the beast with their backs to it as if to stand guard. The others immediately started cutting away at the dinosaur with crude stone knives.

"Look at that," Jared said. "They might not be so bad after all. I guess they were just hungry. I can respect that."

"They're not aggressive," Gear said. "Good. We don't need that many enemies while waiting for rescue."

"We'd be safe in the Intruder," Rat said.

"True, but we don't want them to jack with us in the Intruder before help arrives," Gear said. "We don't know how many are out there. They might come back in large numbers and attack the aircraft. They could make our wait really uncomfortable."

"What do you suggest we do?" Jared asked. His gut didn't give him a clear path forward this time. The enemy wasn't a full-fledged enemy, and the young man didn't have a reputation for his diplomatic skills.

"I got it," Markus said. "Let's give them a gift—a peace offering—something to show them we mean no harm. If we're not a threat, they may leave us alone."

"You want to give them some MREs?" Jared asked. "That might make them kill all of us."

"No…How about my knife?" Markus said. He reached by his side and pulled out the six-inch blade. Black epoxy powder covered the well-balanced blade. "It's a tool they'll know how to use. They won't have anything that can cut like this."

"The man has a point," Gear said.

Bad air exited Jared's lungs with a huge sigh. "Okay. I don't know why I'm giving in to this. I guess I have to trust that other people can be right, too. Go ahead…but one sign of trouble, get back here. We'll go all Metallica and Kill 'Em All!"

Markus handed his rifle over to Jared, raised his shoulders, and straightened his back. He forced a smile as he did for grade school photos. Holding the knife handle first in his left hand, he raised his right as a sign of friendship.

"You got this, Markus," Rat said and gave a thumbs up.

The pilot stepped forward in slow, even steps. His eyes darted about for any sign of danger.

Three cavemen standing before the T. rex looked at each other and nodded. The larger one in the middle spread his open palms outward from his hips.

"That's a good sign," Gear said. "I think we're making progress."

"What's the hand sign for *Get the frick out of here and leave us alone*?" Jared asked. Markus' approach reminded him of a young ring bearer at a wedding.

"He's almost there," Gear said.

Markus stopped a couple of feet in front of the presumed leader. He bowed his head slightly and stretched out his hand with the knife for the man to take by the handle.

The caveman eyed the gift momentarily, then grasped the handle and brought it up for inspection. He moved it up and down a few times as if testing its weight and balance. With a look of curiosity, he brought a finger from his other hand and touched the flat of the blade from the base to the tip. He then fingered the tip and quickly pulled his hand back after obviously finding it very sharp.

"We call that a knife. It's made of steel. Steel is like rock, only a lot harder," Markus said.

The man on the leader's right held out his hand, showing it was his turn with the gift. He received it blade first and grabbed it a little too hard. The knife fell to the ground, and the caveman smeared blood on his hand with his thumb as it pooled from the fresh cut. Undeterred, he picked the knife back up and approached the T. rex.

The others had cut select portions of the dinosaur and were in the process of heading back to the woods with the harvest.

The caveman with the knife went to the T. rex's backside and cut a slice through hide and meat. The ease of the job showed as his face lit up in delight. He then jabbed the blade down straight in and cut out a plug of meat.

"I feel like I'm witnessing a version of Two Thousand and One, A Space Odyssey," Gear said.

"Why?" Jared said.

"We are advancing a civilization to another level through superior technology," Gear said.

The caveman strutted proudly, holding the knife high in one hand and the meat in another. He then returned to the leader's side.

"Okay, it's yours to keep. I'm just going back there with my friends, and you can get on with your Tyrannosaurus cookout," Markus said.

The leader grabbed his arm before Markus could turn and leave, pulling him back to his chest. The other arm went around the pilot's neck.

"Frick!" Jared cried.

The three soldiers raised their weapons to fire. But the leader dragged Markus back by the T. rex, and several other cavemen ran to the forefront and started throwing spears, clubs, and rocks.

"Don't shoot," Jared said. "They have Markus."

The incoming missiles rained down. Instinctually, the team members had to retreat. Jared took a hit from a rock on his left shoulder and felt a club hit him in the back. "Let's get to the Intruder."

"But Markus!" Rat said. "We don't leave men behind."

"If we're dead, there won't be anyone left to get him," Jared said.

The team had put enough distance between them for the second volley of weapons to fall short.

Realizing the cavemen were not pursuing, Jared called them to a halt. "Everybody okay?" He then noticed Gear's blood-soaked left arm.

"Spear nicked me," Gear said.

"Got hit by a few rocks," Rat said. "One hit me in the head, but it missed my face."

"Yeah. Couldn't do much damage by hitting your head," Jared said.

"I'm aware of the situation, Captain," Hammer said over the radio. "Orders?"

Jared looked onward at the departing cavemen. Markus hid in the masses. He could only hope they could rescue him before being harmed. "Hammer, you got a lock on Markus?"

"Yes," Hammer said. "We should be able to trace him as long as they don't damage the transmitter or take him farther than a hundred miles."

"Well, that's the plan, then," Jared said. "We'll travel by night, go all stealth and stuff. We'll get him back, or we won't make it back either."

"One problem with that, *amigo*," Gear said. He pointed up toward the sun. "It's still high noon. I don't think tonight will ever come."

CHAPTER 9

"What infernal place do we find ourselves?" Kolya said. The man had led his team through thick woods filled with trees without typical leaves like the Khimki Forest. The foliage was more akin to palm leaves, ferns, and some that resembled pine needles. They were no closer to a destination than when they had started. The pilot was hot and sweating profusely. He wondered if he had a fever—a gift perhaps from the savage beast who had attacked him and killed his comrade, Sasha. At least the worst of the throbbing in his forearm had subsided. His left hand had also loosened up a bit, and his fingers moved with less effort.

The forest echoed with strange noises and high shrieks. Small, two-legged, lizard-looking animals scurried away every few meters. Fortunately, nothing was as terrible as they had encountered earlier.

Fearing he should not take another step, he stopped the team for a rest. Kolya raised a fist, slunk over to the trunk of a large tree, and sat. He removed his cap and wiped the sweat from his forehead.

Misha opened a duffle bag. He gathered protein bars, split them in half, and handed one to each soldier.

"We are walking in circles," Vanya said. He pulled the paper from the bar and let it fall to the ground.

"How would you know?" Dima said and ate some of his rations. "The compasses do not work." He paused to chew. "The sun never moves in the sky."

"You at least agree we do not know where we are going," Vanya said.

"Yes, but I am not working against a common goal," Dima said. "Perhaps you can lead us to safety." His words sounded more like a threat than an invitation.

The older man shrugged. "It is not my place to lead. My responsibility is to follow orders and ensure their perfect completion. That is why I have seen so much war and still live."

Misha had shared his canteen with Kolya, who had finished his portion of supplies, and sat next to him. "We are bound to find a clearing at some point. There must be at least a river or lake."

"We will continue our path for another two hours, and then we will rest," Kolya said. He locked gazes with Vanya and said, "Those are my orders."

Vanya sipped from his canteen and replaced the cap. "Then I am ready to follow."

Misha jumped to his feet and lowered a hand for Kolya to take, which the leader gladly took.

His legs felt weak initially, but after a few deep breaths, Kolya felt somewhat refreshed. He lifted his rifle and slung it over his shoulder. "Comrades, forward." The few moments of rest were just what he needed.

Another half hour passed. Kolya thought his imagination, or wishful thinking, was playing tricks on his eyes. The woods started to thin, and the canopy overhead opened more to the sunlight beating down on them. Even the air changed. It smelled lighter, cleaner, and less heavy with humidity and rotting forest funk.

"We are coming to a clearing." Kolya turned and said, "Everyone fan out...two meters apart. We will approach side by side."

The soldiers formed their positions and maneuvered past the trees as the obstacles presented themselves.

Above, a greenish-tan pterosaur circled overhead in a spiral, shrieking as it descended. It was such an unusual sight that the team stopped to observe.

"That is not a bird," Misha said. "The wings are bat-like. But it is not a mammal. It has a long bird-like beak. But it is not a bird. Look at that head. It is a creature like I used to draw when I was a child in school—a flying reptile. A Pterodactyl."

"It is attacking," Vanya said and raised his rifle.

"Hold your fire," Kolya said. "We should not call unwanted attention to ourselves unless forced."

The pterosaur's wings spanned at least three meters and looked more ominous as it approached. Then, Kolya saw the creature's destination: a nest high in a tree awaited.

It flapped its wings rapidly, resting in the bowl of odd sticks and grasses. Then, the nest sang songs of hungry offspring eager to eat what their mother had brought.

The show was over, and Kolya motioned the team to move forward until they finally reached a clearing. The scenery opened up like something from the movies—flat grassy land peppered with clumps of trees sprawled in front of them. A majestic mountain range in the distance seemed to almost curve upward into the sky. A body of water glistened not far away, and creatures of various sizes meandered about. Some drinking and some dining on foliage from the trees growing nearby.

"We have traveled back in time," Dima said. "That is the only explanation."

"Perhaps we are still in our time," Vanya said. "We went down over the North Pole. Who knows? This may be a hidden place. A special valley. It is not possible to travel back in time."

Kolya did not have an answer. He did not need one at the moment. It was his job to rescue his team from this situation. The mountains in the distance would provide a high point from which to locate help. But the odd way the mountains looked gave him a sinking feeling in his stomach that the conventional wisdom he had learned may not apply here. His team may not have gone back in time, but they may no longer be on the Earth he knew. Either way, the path was not as straightforward as he had hoped.

A huge greenish-yellow beast lumbered into view. At first, Kolya's mind told him it was a rhinoceros of giant proportions. But the sons of Africa had no place in this strange land. It was a dinosaur—one of the more popularly known to most—a Triceratops.

It had a beak-like mouth, two brow horns above its eyes, and a smaller horn jutting from its nose. A bony frill fanned the top of its head. He estimated it to be over three meters tall and at least thirty meters long. It carried its mass on four legs and appeared more interested in the foliage it ate than anything else.

"I wonder how dangerous it is," Dima said.

"It is a plant eater and not a meat eater," Kolya said. "That must be of some advantage. Perhaps if we leave it alone, it will leave us alone."

Something broke the spell of watching the dinosaur. It was a sound or a vibration, faint at first but then distinct. A large brownish creature standing on two legs and dragging a thick tail entered the scene. The mouth on its enormous head opened and uttered a sound that froze Kolya's spine. Its big, clawed feet plowed toward the Triceratops while short arms bounced in front of its chest. The reddish-brown skin had darker brown markings down its back. There was no mistaking that this dinosaur was a Tyrannosaurus rex.

The Triceratops lifted its mighty head toward the threat and sounded its warning.

The T. rex checked its advance just before reaching the ceratopsian and veered to the side. It opened its monstrous mouth, showing rows of sharp, jagged teeth, and hissed.

The Triceratops was shorter than the T. rex but considerably longer. Even though it did not have teeth, its beak looked like it could cut the rex's leg in two with one bite. The Triceratops lowered its head and quickly brought it back up, using the horns to ward off the attacker.

The T. rex backstepped and hissed. Then stepped toward the grass eater and bit empty air near its head. The brow horns narrowly missed the rex's mouth, and the dinosaur retreated a few meters.

Trying to gain a rear advantage, the T. rex circled the Triceratops. The four-legged creature was considerably agile for its size, using its five-toed feet to pivot and keeping its armored head pointed at the predator.

The T. rex was relentless and attacked again in vain. But the Triceratops hit its target by jutting its head forward and digging its horns in the rex's gut.

With arms up in surprise, the rex thrashed its head and tail about enough to wiggle free. Red blood oozed down the side of its stomach where the horns had penetrated.

The spiky teeth of the T. rex chomped down on one of the brow horns, and the Triceratops struggled to pull free. The T. rex didn't waiver and held fast through its victim's cries, twisting its head about until the horn snapped at the base.

Backing away, the Triceratops kept its head up, warning the rex it wasn't ready to surrender the fight.

Nevertheless, the T. rex lunged forward with another crushing bite on one side of the Triceratops' frill. Crunching bone intermingled with the brays of the grass eater. Somehow, it freed itself again, but its movements were less sure. There was no hiding the Triceratops was injured, and the T. rex's aggression grew.

Another chomp toward the Triceratops' head made it twist to the side to avoid it, exposing the back of its neck.

Sensing victory, the T. rex's jaws opened wide and bit behind the frill. Blood squirted like a crushed tomato. The Triceratops moaned as loud as an air horn and thrashed its squatty body about.

The T. rex held firm, twisting its head from side to side until the grass eater went still. It pulled back and came away with a hunk of blood-dripping meat. Lifting back its head, the dinosaur swallowed the first fruit of its victory and returned to satisfy its hunger.

The commotion was enough to rouse the interest of several other species of dinosaurs meandering about the area. Fresh kill was available, and it was first come, first served. A gathering of pterosaurs circled overhead. A few dinosaurs that resembled the T. rex slunk toward the feast. The Moros were much smaller—about the size of a human. Their heads were more lizard-like, and the teeth were not as threatening. Several smaller bipedal dinosaurs, the same kind they had come upon in the forest, joined in. The Compsognathus were the size of modern-day chickens.

"This will provide the distraction we need to move on," Kolya said.

Several Compsognathus scurried over to the carcass, ignoring the towering T. rex. The animals started feeding, taking small bites, and sometimes challenging a companion for space at the table. If the T. rex's next bite became too close for comfort, the creatures would scatter and make loud chirping noises.

The larger Moros received a threatening hiss from the T. rex as it became apparent that they wanted to share. Still, the dinosaurs maintained their quest and eventually ate.

Smaller pterosaurs left the tops of trees and landed on the back of the Triceratops, where they began pecking away for food.

"The dinosaurs are far enough away that I do not think we will be noticed," Kolya said. "We will keep low to the ground—and head to that other grouping of trees." He pointed toward the destination with his rifle barrel.

"And then?" Vanya asked.

"And then we shall make our way to the mountains," Kolya said.

"I have never seen mountains like those," Vanya said. "There is something wrong with this place."

"It is as if the world curves in the wrong direction," Dima said. "As if we are on the inside."

Kolya had trouble defining what was different about this new land. But Dima had put his feelings into words, unbelievable as they sounded. It made sense that they were inside a world rather than on the outside. The sun above provided heat and light, but it was not the sun—the star—of the planet of his birth. Could it be that they were inside of the Earth now? Stories of a hollow Earth were creations of movies and novels, not real life. Yet, it was impossible to deny reality.

"What about water?" Vanya asked. "Our supply is limited."

"We have plenty for now. There is too much activity in this area to risk getting it from the lake," Kolya said. "We will leave." He didn't waste any time and lowered his shoulders before trotting toward his destination.

The trees were less than one hundred meters away. As the team approached, a gigantic four-legged dinosaur appeared to one side with an extremely long, thick neck and equally long tail. The head was small compared to its body size, with nostrils sitting unusually high on top. Its legs were as thick as massive tree trunks, and Kolya felt as if he could run underneath upright and not touch the belly of the beast.

If his comrades had any concerns, they kept them to themselves. Perhaps the early reservations about accepting his leadership were waning.

At one point, the Apatosaurus turned its attention toward them. It chewed lazily on a mouthful of foliage without concern and returned to eat more when finished.

The pterosaurs high in the treetops announced the team's arrival. Kolya had hoped stealth would be on their side, but they were out of place and a potential threat. He kept his gaze sharp, watching for any number of predators that may only be a few steps away. It was then that he worried about their water supply. Conservatively, they had enough for another day. Then, he realized he was about to fall into the trap of self-doubt. No leader worth command veered from the plan unless forced to do so.

After twenty minutes of traveling through the sparsely timbered area, the landscape opened for several hundred meters, dotted with more patches of woods. The mountains seemed no closer than before. He considered resting now but thought it best to make it to the next wooded area because he noticed how signs of animal life diminished farther away from the body of water.

He turned to his comrades and said, "When we reach the next grouping of trees, we will secure a space and take turns resting." Kolya motioned ahead with his right hand, and the team moved forward.

Vanya caught up to his right side—almost as if the older man were trying to take the lead. Misha kept his stride a few steps behind Kolya, and Dima dutifully trailed in the rear to protect their backside.

Sweat rolled down his forehead. The anticipation of reaching the next refuge became as strong as his growing thirst.

As the pace of each step became like the growing beat of a drum, a shadow from above covered the team and darkened the ground in front of them. Kolya instinctively looked up and at first thought a low-flying plane was overhead. It quickly became apparent that no such modern invention was there to save them.

SKEER-AK!

A massive flying reptile of unimaginable proportions soared past. Its wingspan was at least ten meters, and its neck was longer than its body. Huge claws hung from the rear end of the brownish-colored creature. The beak on its triangular-shaped head was large enough to engulf a full-grown man, and the green crown on its head looked out of place as if painted.

Kolya brought his men to a halt to watch the spectacle. They were lucky not to have been the victims of an unexpected attack. As the Quetzalcoatlus moved farther away, he saw why. Ahead, moving past the timbered area some fifty meters before them, a group of men carrying a carcass on a pole walked into an open area.

Fatigue had weakened Kolya's eyesight, and he struggled to focus on the discovery of fellow humans in this strange land. There may have been eight to twelve in the group. It was impossible for him to tell if or how well they were armed.

"We are not alone," Vanya said. He lifted his rifle and stared into the scope. "Nine men. Spears. Bows. Possibly knives on their sides. No match for us."

"Are they a match for the beast attacking them?" Dima asked, taking a position next to Kolya.

"We need them alive—to help us!" Misha said with hope in his voice.

The Quetzalcoatlus landed several meters from the men. It used its front arms, which supported the wings as front legs, and the pointed wing tips folded neatly away from the ground.

"It can walk. The neck is three meters long. It looks like a giraffe," Misha said.

The reptile looked more like it would be at home in a Japanese Kaiju movie than in any zoo Kolya had been.

SKEER-AK! After the cry, the creature stuck out its neck and snapped its beak against empty air as its target threw itself backward.

Two men poked long spears at its body, careful to avoid the deadly head. Two others loaded bows and sent arrows flying toward it.

The beast's mighty jaws snared one unlucky warrior. His yells of pain were loud enough to reach Kolya's ears. It was time to make their move.

"Let's kill this monster," Kolya said, running full speed toward the fray. The others followed.

Vanya was the first to stop. He sighted his rifle and squeezed off two shots.

Misha crashed to one knee and let a series of rounds ring out.

The bullets definitely affected the Quetzalcoatlus. It dropped its prey, stopped its attack, and turned to face its new adversaries. In a fury, it shrieked its warning and shuffled forward on its eerie winged arms and clawed feet.

Some warriors tended to their injured or dead companion. The arrows continued to fly from the archers.

Kolya and Dima braked some eight meters from the creature, adding to the barrage from the other comrades.

The Quetzalcoatlus' head flailed about as blood-splattered holes peppered its chest. It raised its arm and unfolded its wings as if to take flight, but it was useless. Its body shuddered, and its head wavered as the neck could no longer support it. When it collapsed to the ground, the excitement that seemed to electrify the air gave way to an empty calm.

The beast defeated, Kolya raised a hand for the comrades to join him.

The arrows had stopped, and the warriors looked toward them with great curiosity.

The team approached the dead pterosaur to keep it between them and their new acquaintances. "Do not make any sudden moves," Kolya said in a low voice. "We cannot afford to scare away our first and perhaps only chance at a rescue."

"I will kill the first who attacks," Vanya said. "Sometimes the death of one will send fear into the hearts of others who would dare to try."

Kolya took a long breath and didn't waste his energy addressing Vanya. It was up to him to make a successful first contact.

A young man had emerged from the group. He was relatively clean and wore a vest of what looked like animal skin. A different type of animal skin covered his loins. Colored beads hung from around his neck. From his clean-shaven face, Kolya deduced the man to be in his early twenties.

Kolya stopped by the head of the Quetzalcoatlus and marveled at the size. He thought how wonderful it would have been to have a photograph of the team in front of it—but no one would believe it to be real. And now was not the time for this fantastic adventure to distract him from his mission. "Keep the guns pointing at the ground. Shoot if I am attacked—only then." He slowly stepped away from the pterosaur while shouldering his rifle. His elbows stayed by his side, and both hands with open palms led the way in what he hoped was a universal sign of *I come in peace*.

The men standing behind the young leader moved closer to him as Kolya neared. Everyone kept silent, and no one threatened violence.

Two meters apart, Kolya stopped and said clearly, "Hello." He was then close enough to notice the spearheads were made of metal, most resembling copper.

The men looked at him curiously, like a child who didn't understand. He expected this because the odds did not favor their understanding of Russian.

The leader brought his palms up before him, imitating Kolya, and said, "*Bawo.*"

This certainly seemed like progress. However, many hours of exchange would be necessary before communicating on a common level. "My…name…is…Kolya. Kolya." He then poked a finger to his chest. "Kol-ya."

Likewise, the leader pointed to himself and said, "*Gamba.*"

Kolya pointed again to himself and said, "Kolya." Then, pointed to the leader and said, "Gamba."

The exchange brought smiles and nods of approval from the warriors. Kolya turned his gaze to his comrades and saw they were ready to progress now that the initial fear of combat had passed. He pointed to them and said, "Men. Kolya's men." He pointed to Gamba. "Kolya and men. Go…with Gamba." He used both hands and motioned toward the warriors. "Go with Gamba. Home. Home."

The warriors spoke among themselves in a language that did not seem primitive, and the conversation was free of abrupt emotion. The group hushed, and Gamba said, "*Wa si abule mi.*" He pointed toward a forest. "*Abule.*"

Sensing his message was understood, he waved his men over.

Then he turned his attention to the injured man on the ground. It was apparent from his crushed chest that he was no longer alive. But then he noticed something strange. At first, it did not register in his mind, but then it became undeniable. The animal carcass hanging from a pole was not supported by a man on each end. It hung in empty air. The only items of note were a band of black material with a strange goldish glow on each end.

A pit grew in Kolya's stomach. He felt more lost now than ever.

CHAPTER 10

The crew was inside the Intruder. The sense of urgency to rescue Markus was palpable.

"I can't reach Markus on the radio," Hammer said. "The Neanderthals must have taken his goggles. He's still moving, though. Good sign." He turned to Rat and said, "Help me with the backpacks."

"I thought you said the spear just nicked you?" Jared asked as he cleaned the wound on Gear's left deltoid. "This cut runs deep."

"Rat, before you help Hammer, grab the superglue and get over here," Jared said.

The young man did as ordered and arrived with the bonding agent.

"I'm going to hold the skin together, and you need to squirt this stuff over the top. Don't get any on my fingers, or Gear and I will have to double-date for the rest of our lives."

Rat closed his left eye, opened his mouth, and stuck his tongue to the left side as he squeezed out a ribbon of glue on the wound.

"Okay, that's enough for now." Jared blew on the glue to harden it. After a minute or so, he said, "Put some more on it."

Rat complied and returned the cap to the glue when he finished.

"There, good as new," Jared said as he wiped his hands on his pants. "Uh, Gear. I'm going to let you stay here and guard the Intruder."

"Why? You said I was good." Gear had grabbed a fresh shirt and gently slipped his injured arm into a sleeve.

Jared shrugged his shoulders. "Hammer is the weapons guy. I can't leave Rat here by himself. It'd be like that movie "Home Alone"…but with dinosaurs, not burglars."

"As you wish, *amigo*," Gear said, turning his attention toward the pilot console.

"You know, Gear, sometimes when you say *amigo*, I distinctly hear *asshole*," Jared said.

The tall Mexican with polished white teeth and perfect hair broke a rare smile but remained silent.

"Is Markus still on the move?" Hammer asked. He zipped up a backpack and tossed it toward Rat.

"It looks like it," Gear said. "Almost two miles away."

"There're too many of them," Hammer said. "We'll have to depend on stealth."

"I probably got more brains in my little finger than all of the cavemen put together," Rat said as he threaded his arms through the backpack straps.

"Neanderthals were intelligent. Maybe not on the same level as Homo sapiens. But they are surviving here by just using crude weapons," Gear said. "Strength-wise, Neanderthals were superior to Homo sapiens."

"We won't have to worry about hand-to-hand combat. We'll go in with our meta-cloaks, and poof, make Markus disappear," Hammer said.

"Which means we'll have to wear our tactical helmets to work with the Harry Potter cloaks of invisibility when we put them on," Jared said. "Good thing those helmets have little fans to help keep us cool in this heat."

The three men gathered equipment and double-checked that everything was in place and ready to go.

Jared put on his tactical helmet and said, "Luke, I am your father."

Gear closed his eyes and shook his head. "Do you have to say that every time you put that on?"

"Luke, I am your *amigo*," Jared said.

Gear paused a moment and said, "I hate that too."

"Potato—po-tot-oe," Jared said.

"Guys, Markus isn't getting any closer," Hammer said. "Let's move out."

"Be careful," Gear said as he observed the screen. "Lots of activity by the T. rex carcass."

The door dropped at the rear of the Intruder, and Hammer was the first one out. Rat followed, with Jared filing out next.

Once Jared and the team exited the aircraft's shelter, he saw pterosaurs circling above. There was a lot of commotion around what remained of the T. rex, so he zoomed in on the scene.

Small, two-legged lizard-like dinosaurs frenziedly fed on raw flesh. A couple of dinosaurs, like the ones they had killed earlier—Troodons—battled over a chunk of meat. Their heads snaked back and forth—lunging—but not connecting with anything. Finally, one bit into the meat, only to have the other chomp down on it, too. The Troodons struggled in a tug-of-war until the piece of flesh tore apart. At that point, the dinosaurs ran in opposite directions with their prizes.

"Man, that is some gross stuff there," Rat said.

A pterosaur dove from above and landed on a small portion of what remained of the tail. It grabbed it with its claws and struggled to take flight. A bird-like dinosaur half the size of a man quickly snatched it and pulled the pterosaur to the ground, shrieking and flapping its wings until it could right itself and take flight.

"Eh, I've seen worse at the Golden Corral Buffet on Saturday nights," Jared said.

"Let's go by the river. We'll follow it until we reach the woods and return to Markus' trail. Those dinosaurs are too occupied with the kill for them to worry about us," Hammer said.

"I like the way you think," Jared said. "Lead the way."

Jared kept one eye on the feeding frenzy and one on the river. They were twenty feet or so away from the bank, and he feared something slithering up might catch them by surprise.

A fin resembling a sail emerged from the middle of the river. Jared zoomed in and saw it had to belong to a dinosaur. "Gear, what am I looking at?"

"Just a second," Gear said over the radio. "My guess is it's a Spinosaurus."

"Spinosaurus," Jared said. "That sounds bad. How big is it?"

"Forty—fifty feet," Gear said. "Stay out of the water, and you'll be okay."

"I feel like I'm in a prehistoric zoo, and I'm a walking Happy Meal," Jared said.

"Hey, look over on the other side of the bank. It's one of those silver poles like Markus and I saw when we went by the river," Rat said.

"Yeah, I heard you two talking about it," Hammer said. He stared at it briefly and said, "I've zoomed in on it. Its signature shows it's made of aluminum. It does look out of place here."

"We ain't got time to worry about that," Jared said. "It's the lions and tigers and bears we need to concentrate on."

The flat ground gave way to the dark forest. At least the trees provided shade from the unrelenting rays of this world's sun. But now every tree hid a potential death behind it—out of the frying pan and into the fire. It didn't matter. They were going to return with Markus or not return at all.

"Gear, give us directions," Hammer said over the radio.

"Start heading at a forty-five-degree angle from where you are facing. Markus hasn't moved for about ten minutes. They are resting, or they have reached the Neanderthals' home," Gear said.

"Ten-four," Hammer said. "How far away?"

"Around a couple of miles as a crow flies."

"We can try to make it within an hour," Hammer said. "Just keep us heading in the right direction."

"Ten-four."

Hammer turned his gaze to Jared, and the captain gave him a nod of approval.

The eerie sounds of the deep woods increased with each step. Shrieks from pterosaurs and only God knows what else echoed against odd moans and brays of not-so-far-away creatures. Something in the earthy funk irritated the back of Jared's throat. Small two-legged dinosaurs popped up often. The creatures would stop, turn their head from side to side, and run away. Apparently, they were sizing them up for dinner, but deciding a fight might not go their way. Which was a blessing, as Jared didn't want to use their weapons unless they had to. He thought he might be able to stomp one to death if attacked but didn't want to put that to the test.

Over half an hour had passed when a slow growl, heavy on bass, abruptly stopped the team.

The three brought their rifle barrels up and scanned the area for the threat.

"I don't see anything," Rat said.

"It came from that direction," Hammer pointed ahead to the left.

The growl sounded again.

"That was behind us," Jared said.

"Are you sure?" Rat said with some excitement in his voice.

"Could be two," Hammer said.

"Or more!" Rat said.

"Calm down," Jared said. "We'll get them before they get us. We're going to advance slowly. Set your aim to auto. If anything looks like Barney the dinosaur or one of his cousins, shoot it."

Something moved through the forest toward them, rattling leaves and snapping wood with each step.

"I think—" Rat started.

When the dinosaur howled, it shook Jared to the core. A numbing coolness dripped down his spine. The captain had experienced heavy combat before. Had battled hand-to-hand in the caves of Afghanistan and still lived. But nothing he had faced in the past matched the terror he felt now.

Then, it came toward him at a speed he wasn't prepared for. This wasn't like a deer hunt, where you waited to kill an unaware animal who would run at the first sign of a threat. This beast was the hunter, undeterred in an environment that gave it all the advantages.

Hammer squeezed off two rounds, and Rat followed with one.

Jared couldn't get a clear shot with the other two between him and the dinosaur. It was about the size of a large man—with two legs and a tail that stretched around six feet behind it. The lizard-like head was nothing like a T. rex's. It looked evil. Pissed off. And like it was going to kill them or die trying.

The monster ran behind a big tree right in front and came charging.

Hammer and Rat took a step back, which led Jared to retreat as well. The two began firing in rapid succession.

A growl behind Jared had him spinning on his heels. He turned just in time to see a second dinosaur poke out its head and chomp down on his rifle barrel. He held it tightly, but the Dilophosaurus jerked its head backward and pulled it from his grasp.

Jared ended up face-first on the forest floor. The next thing he knew was that something had latched onto his backpack, and he was being dragged away.

"Hey! Help!" He looked up and saw the black claws dangling above from short arms and even more deadly claws on the feet.

The Dilophosaurus' jaws released the backpack, and Jared rolled to his side before the creature struck his tactical helmet. Unable to penetrate the carbon fibers, it let out a yell and pulled its head back—ready for another assault.

Jared watched as his teammates' rounds found their target and sent parts of the Dilophosaurus exploding in the air like meat fireworks. The beast trembled uncontrollably and collapsed, never to rise again.

"Jared, are you hurt?" Hammer asked.

The captain sat up and then stood. He brushed away rotting foliage and dirt from his shirt. "Ain't nothing hurt but my pride. I might need a change of underwear, but nothing is broken or bleeding. I'm good."

"Man, that was close," Rat said. He stepped over the dead dinosaur and used his rifle barrel to lift the lips to see the teeth. "If that thing would have bitten you…"

"I believe your encounter was with a Dilophosaurus," Gear said over the radio. "Dinosaurs sometimes hunt in pairs or groups. You're lucky there were only two."

"Here, I'd rather be lucky than rich," Jared said. "How far are we from Markus?"

"You were making good time," Gear said. "Less than half a mile. Keep heading in the direction you were going. I would guess you'd be able to see their village well before you get there."

"We're still in heavy woods," Jared said. "Unless these Neanderthals live in trees like Tarzan, I suspect we'll be out soon."

Jared nodded, and Hammer led the way.

Less than ten minutes had passed when the forest thinned. Part of the terrain beyond brought back memories of Jared's trip to the Mojave Desert. A mountain of rock stretched across the left side of the landscape. Zooming in, tents made of animal skins that resembled teepees of Native Indians dotted the flat ground away from the mountain. There were trees here and there. A large parcel of land on the right side of the landscape was green and appeared to have rows. "I see white people."

"Must be hundreds of them…from the number of tents," Hammer said. "They're advanced enough to have agriculture."

"What kind of culture do Agris have?" Rat asked.

"Boy, don't tell me you really just asked that?" Jared said.

"What?" Rat said.

"Agriculture means *farming*, Rat," Gear said.

"Oh. Then why didn't he say farming then?" Rat said.

"You're right," Hammer said. He shook his head and said as if to himself, "And my mom used to call *me* retarded."

"Captain," Gear said over the radio. "I've got a fix on you and Markus. Sending over the grid that paints his location."

"Copy that," Jared said. His screen switched to a grid pattern, with the tent housing his pilot flashing a red dot.

"He's on the outside of the village. Good. It'd be a lot harder if he were stuck in the middle," Hammer said.

Several tents, serving as what Jared assumed were outposts, fronted the main village by at least fifty yards. Each had a two-man team with weapons nearby. Surprisingly, while he was zoomed in, he saw that an aluminum pole, like the ones by the river, was present at each outpost. "More of those poles by the outposts."

"Maybe there're land makers—like a survey team plants," Hammer said.

"Maybe," Jared said. "But for now, what's the plan?"

"We'll go around the last tent on the left—close to the rock formation," Hammer said. "I'd feel better if it were night, but we'll be far enough away that no one will see us."

"Magic time," Jared said.

The crew removed their backpacks and retrieved their Metamaterial cloaks.

Rat struggled to get his backpack back on and said, "This thing is going to be hot." He then draped the cloak around his back and closed the snaps from the neck on down.

"I'd rather the heat than the cold," Jared said while adjusting his cloak.

"We'll arch over to the left and get well past the outpost before heading to the tent," Hammer said.

"Ready," Jared said.

"Good," Rat said.

"Follow me, boys," Hammer said. "We got one shot at this and can't afford to blow it."

"You had me at blow," Jared said.

"You don't miss an opportunity to be an ass, do you?" Hammer asked. He started at a fast pace and headed toward the mountain.

"Hammer, you complete me," Jared said, quickly catching up with the weapons officer.

"Enough with the Jerry Maguire routine," Hammer said. "I'm not a Tom Cruise fan."

"Those Mission Impossibles are some badass, though," Rat said. "Hey, Jared."

"What?"

"I've always wondered how a man like yourself never picked up a nickname," Rat said.

"Some have tried, but I don't let any names stick. Jared is one of the best names a man can have," Jared said. "Think of those Jared Jewelry commercials. They have a psychological effect on the ladies. You know, *enjoy the gift of giving at Jared. More than a gift, at Jared. He got it at Jared.* You can't think of my name without thinking of expensive jewelry. Ladies like jewelry—so ladies like Jared Belazaire."

"Still, I think a nickname would be way cooler," Rat said.

"Well, I wanted *Ladies Love Cool Jared*, but someone had already taken LL Cool J," Jared said. "Besides, it's the name my mother gave me. It sure is better than having a nickname like Gym Rat."

As the three marched on, Jared became increasingly worried. The cloak was most effective at night, as Hammer said, or from long distances during the day. They were good for now but must come in close contact to rescue Markus. Stealth would be the only way to do that. Perhaps the Neanderthals had a sleeping schedule where the majority would bed down at the same time. That would better the odds. But how long would they have to wait before knowing the best move forward? Time might not be on their side. For all he knew, the cavemen were putting salt and pepper on Markus and wood on the fire for the cookout.

The sun had the inside of the cloak hot enough to bake cookies. Jared wanted relief from his canteen but could not drink while wearing the tactical helmet. He wondered if astronauts could drink water while in full spacesuits. If so, it was time for Command to upgrade their gear.

More time had passed, and they were nearing the point where they would approach the village. The closest tent was a few minutes away.

"Team," Hammer said. "I think we're close enough to make our move. I don't see anyone on the outskirts. The main activity seems to be in the middle of the village. Markus is a prisoner, so there'll be guards. We'll use our pistols with the tranquilizers to knock them out. We'll hide Markus behind us and lead him away. Be patient, and let's make this happen."

The three spread six feet apart and stepped toward the village. They were slow and steady, giving the Metamaterials light-bending and reflection properties time to adjust without distortion. The first tent was less than twenty feet away. Thermal imaging didn't show anyone inside. In minutes, they would reach Markus.

As Jared scanned the area, he saw two Neanderthals from one outpost had left and were heading toward them. Could they see them? Had the dinosaur damaged his cloak when it chomped down on the backpack? "Team, we got company!"

"Don't move," Hammer said.

The three froze.

Jared zoomed in on the two natives and saw them sniffing the air. "Great. I don't know if they can see us...but it looks like they can smell us."

The two ran, heading straight for them and yelping a warning in high-pitched voices.

Suddenly, several Neanderthals came pouring from around the tents and poking their primitive weapons toward the sky. They, too, sniffed the air and headed straight for them.

"They're too close," Hammer said. "We can't outrun them. Captain?"

"Get your vomit grenades," Jared said. "Let's see if we can put these cavemen on their knees, puking their guts out long enough for us to get Markus."

"Sounds like a plan," Rat said.

By this time, the Neanderthals were close enough almost to reach out and touch Hammer. They had perplexed looks on their faces. Some squinted and opened and closed their eyes as if trying to focus.

"Okay, on three, pull the pin, drop them, and kick them out under the cloak toward our hairy buddies. One, two, three."

The grenades emitted their sickening frequency, and Jared heard the noise cancellation kick in. To his surprise, the cavemen didn't react at all. One of them picked up a grenade and examined it. He then shook it and tried to take a bite of it. Not sure of what he had, he thought it valuable enough to keep it.

"They aren't working," Jared said.

"Neanderthal inner ear structure differs slightly from humans. My guess is just enough where the frequency doesn't affect them like us. I doubt the Jackass grenades would work either," Gear said over the radio.

This was the worst position Jared had ever found himself in. They could take out everyone around them in short order, but the number of Neanderthals in the village would outlast their bullets. "Gear, I don't know what will happen, but I've decided not to fight. We'll try to outsmart them to keep ourselves alive. You'll have to get us out of here when the rescue jet comes. That is, if we're not dead."

"I can come with a B-F-G and cause enough distraction that you'll be able to escape. Try not to give up your radio. I can leave in five and be there as soon as possible," Gear said.

As good of a plan as it sounded, there would still be too many unknowns. "I like your plan, Gear. But for now, you stay there. When the jet comes, you can try it then."

The caveman closest to Hammer moved his spear slowly until the tip of the stone touched him on his left shoulder.

Hammer twisted his body and knocked the spear aside with his right shoulder.

The Neanderthal was surprised.

"Jared, we need to show ourselves, or they'll poke us to death," Hammer said.

"Okay, the moment of truth has arrived," Jared said. "Let's do it slowly. And if they get nasty…we get nastier."

He unsnapped the front of the cloak and let it fall to the ground. Hammer and Rat did the same.

The cavemen OOHed and AAHed, some taking a few steps backward.

The tactical helmets came off next. Jared held it in his left hand. He took the radio module out and clipped it to the collar of his shirt. Rat and Hammer did the same and slid their rifles off their shoulders—keeping the barrels pointed toward the ground.

Then, the leader they had met earlier arrived with his entourage. He wore Markus' goggles and had the knife he had been given strapped to the side of his loincloth.

"At least he doesn't have Markus' teeth on a necklace," Jared said.

"*Hwái ist þu hēr?*" the leader asked.

"They can talk. I wonder why they didn't when we first met, but I don't speak Swahili," Jared said. "Gear, any idea what he's saying?"

"A-I is checking now," Gear said. "Hmm."

"Hmm, what?" Jared said. We ain't got time for Hmm."

"A-I suggest that the language is similar to Proto-Germanic. I think he's asking why you are there," Gear said.

"Tell him I'm here for my friend," Jared said. He pulled the radio module from his collar and turned on the external speaker.

"*Ik im hēraz furi mina frēundaz,*" the radio transmitted.

The leader eyed the radio held in Jared's hand like it was the most confusing object he had ever seen. He then turned his gaze to his entourage as if he understood but was looking for reinforcements. After a few whispers and grunts between them, the leader said, "*Wē wiljǭną þik tō immai.*"

The radio barked back, *We will take you to him.*

"Well, this is better than I'd hoped," Jared said, clipping the radio back on his shirt collar.

One of the leader's cronies approached Jared and held out his hand. "*Gib mir þata.*" He pointed to the captain's knife.

There was no need for the translator. Markus' knife must have been a prize possession in Neanderthal land. Jared pulled his knife from the sheath and handed it over. "Gas, grass, or ass. I guess no one rides for free."

CHAPTER 11

The Russian elite made the journey toward the village side by side with the humans, save for Vanya, who insisted he bring up the rear and watch for any signs if their new acquaintances had less-than-honorable intentions.

The humans had draped the dead warrior over the pole next to the animal carcass. Kolya was astounded when the pole remained motionless, suspended in the air, even with the sudden addition of the extra weight. How was it that such primitive people had such advanced technology? It only made sense that it did not originate with them. Therefore, where, or even more worrisome, who did it come from? Obviously, they had not found a way to weaponize the anti-gravity material or even use it as propulsion. As fantastic as this discovery was, it meant nothing if they could not find a way back to their world and time.

A few pterosaurs circled overhead but didn't dive and challenge the humans for the kill. Kolya was glad, as he did not want to use more ammo than required. So far, the only forest animals had been small two-legged dinosaurs. Some were curious, but most scurried away in fear of the men.

Gamba and his warriors did not seem concerned about them or the Russians and their weapons. Now that they were in a wooded area, the primitive men were more occupied with traversing the terrain. The trees only added to the difficulty of spotting predators.

The warriors spoke few words to each other, and when they did, they kept them to a whisper. Hand signals became the communication of choice. Two warriors acted as scouts, staying ahead just before getting out of the line of sight—though the trees and brush sometimes hid them.

Kolya felt like he was living in a bad science fiction movie. He might even find the situation amusing if his hunger, thirst, and the miserable heat had not been so intense.

He looked over at Misha. The young man's eyes were wide as saucers as if he were hopped up on amphetamines. Kolya wondered if Misha could keep his cool if attacked by a native creature. Accidentally shooting or killing a warrior might turn the situation entirely negative.

Dima was on the other side of Kolya. A few steps behind. He turned his head and gave the leader a reassuring gaze and a slight nod. It surprised Kolya how that simple gesture lifted his spirits.

He gazed back at Vanya and raised his right thumb. The expected return did not come. Instead, the older soldier's steely eyes conveyed the message that he wanted his leader dead. What would be the gain of that? They were stronger as a team. Perhaps it was just a game Vanya played. Kolya decided not to be manipulated. Turn his emotions off. If Vanya insisted on being obstinate, it might eventually come to fists to clear the differences between them.

A branch above and behind him made a creaking noise. Kolya turned and saw a feathered, two-legged dinosaur fall on Vanya. The animal looked more like a bird than it did a reptile.

The old soldier landed on his back, completely surprised. The theropod's clawed feet pinned his arms down.

"Vanya!" Misha cried. He lifted his rifle to aim.

"No! You'll hit Vanya," Kolya said.

The Dromaeosaurid spread its feathered arms and let out a ferocious hiss.

Gamba and the other warriors rushed over, leading with the tips of their spears. The frontal assault quickly pushed the dinosaur backward and off the Russian soldier. It bit down on one spear and wrestled with its owner. The other warriors surrounded it, each stabbing it with wild abandon. Blood squirted from the wounds and cascaded down its body. The Dromaeosaurid squawked in defiance and sprang on the warrior directly in front. Dropping to one knee, the primitive human placed the butt of the spear securely on the ground—leaving the spear at an angle. The dinosaur impaled itself on the spear directly in the middle of its chest—with the remaining warriors delivering death stabs until all life left the predator.

Misha was already by Vanya's side. "How bad are you hurt?"

The soldier lay with his eyes closed and his mouth open. Then he grimaced and moaned. His eyes blinked open, and he said, "My head...hit the ground hard."

"Do you think you can walk?" Misha asked.

He exhaled loudly and said, "I think so...OHH!" He grabbed his left side with his right hand. "My ribs. May have cracked a few."

"You are bleeding. Sit up, and I will remove your shirt," Misha said.

Blood soaked the left side of Vanya's chest. Misha gingerly removed the man's shirt and examined the wound. "You have a bruise on your chest, and the claw has cut you," Misha said. "I will patch you up." He then dug through his bag and retrieved the medical kit. The antiseptic on the cleaning pad forced a cry from Vanya's lips. Misha applied gauze and taped the wound to stop the bleeding.

Gamba and his warriors watched with great interest. An item so simple as medical tape must have seemed to be the product of magic.

Kolya strode over to Vanya as he pulled himself off the ground. "Will you be able to travel?"

The older soldier cleared his throat and spat as he eased his left arm into his shirt. "What choice have I?"

"I am sure you have noticed the animal carcass is suspended without the aid of the warriors," Kolya said. "If needed, we could pursue a way for you to be carried too."

"I would rather you shoot me here and be done with it," Vanya said.

As tempted as Kolya was to respond threateningly, he decided better. "Let us move on as best we can. I will take the rear position. You and Misha walk with our new friends." He turned his attention to Gamba and nodded.

The leader returned the nod and advanced to the front of the group.

Time trudged along. As strange as it was, the horizon started looking more brown than dull green. Perhaps they were approaching mountains. Finally! A chance to go to a high spot and search for any sign of modern civilization. The opportunity sent a surge of energy through him.

The woods thinned, and they passed an aluminum-looking rounded pipe about a meter tall jutting from the ground, resembling a vehicle block found in parking lots protecting a building. Dima, who had moved to the front of the group, motioned Kolya forward. The leader trotted over to his comrade and could not believe what he saw.

A city resembling what ancient Egypt could have looked like lay ahead. Massive stone structures outlined the perimeter. Green foliage intermingled with other stone buildings and looked more magnificent than Red Square. To the right side of the city, a river flowed, carrying boats with sails. Kolya then felt a breeze kick up. The cool, dry air made him feel like he was back on the Earth he remembered.

"I cannot believe my eyes," Misha said as he sidled beside Kolya. "Magnificent. Look! There is a pyramid at the center of the city."

Gamba and his warriors waited patiently as the Russians gathered and marveled at the metropolis.

"What kind of world are we in?" Dima asked. "We crash-landed in prehistoric times—seventy million years in the past. This city looks only a few thousand years from the twenty-first century. If we travel farther, will we end up back home?"

"I have yet to see any aircraft," Vanya said. "I no longer think we are on our Earth." He grimaced and stretched his left side. "Right now, I only wish for a soft bed and a dark place to sleep."

"I feel like we are closer to home," Misha said.

"Eh, your elbow is close, yet you cannot bite it," Vanya said.

"*O to akoko lati lo*," Gamba said and pointed forward.

"It is time for us to go," Kolya said. "I do not know what the future may hold. Their weapons are primitive, but they can kill nonetheless. We will use our guns only for self-defense. This ultimately means that if we use them, we will die because we will be outnumbered. Let us go and embrace our fate."

CHAPTER 12

Half the village must have gathered around Jared and his crew—men, women, and children. They were behaved, but all were curious. Hands reached out to touch the soldiers. The camouflage print of their uniforms fascinated them.

"Hey…how y'all doing?" Jared said while flashing a big smile. He waved with his right hand and followed behind the tribe leader and his men. "Howdy…nice hair lip…good morning…you must have a hard time eating corn on the cob with those teeth…nice to meet you…you stink, man, do you stink…salami…cheese fries…hello…your breath could stop a train."

Rat and Hammer followed behind, an arm's length apart. They kept their mouths shut and eyes on the alert for danger.

Coming to a stop in front of a teepee made of greenish hide, the Neanderthal leader waited for Jared to catch up. *"Dein Freund ist hier drin."*

Your friend is in here, the radio translated.

Jared turned and looked around. People were so thick he couldn't see beyond them and the other teepees. It could have been a trap, but he had played this hand to win. "Hammer and Rat. You two wait out here and keep an eye on things. This might be a trap to get us all in one place. Here goes nothing."

The chief pulled the flap to the teepee.

Jared took a breath and stepped in.

It was dark, and his eyes hadn't adjusted to the filtered light when he heard:

"Jared! I was wondering what all the commotion was going on outside."

"Markus! Buddy! You okay, man?" Jared asked.

"Hey, I'm fine. For now. How did you get here? Did they capture you, too?" Markus asked.

"It's a long story that we can talk about later. I can tell you that the leader caught us trying to sneak in and did what we asked by bringing us to you. Of course, it cost me my knife. At least we can buy our safety for now. The way they're fascinated with our uniforms, we might have to leave naked," Jared said. He looked around the tent. "You got a bed. Some fruit. And it looks like you didn't finish your T. rex dinner."

"I'm not sure what kind of meat that was. It might have been better had it not been overcooked," Markus said.

"I was worried you might show up on the menu," Jared said.

"No, I don't think they're cannibals. I haven't seen any human skulls or bones decorating the village. From what I can tell, they're fairly civilized," Markus said.

"You said that you were fine for now. What did that mean? Any idea what they had in mind to do with you?" Jared asked.

"Communication's been kinda rough," Markus said. "The leader, they call him Fuhrer—"

"Fuhrer? You mean like that, Heil Hitler bastard?" Jared said while bringing two fingers under his nose to mimic a mustache.

Markus sighed and shrugged. "That's what they call him. I'm no linguist, but their language reminds me of German."

"Old German, Gear said," Jared said. "We can communicate with them with a translator."

"That's fantastic!" Markus said. "Anyway, the leader points to himself and says, *Mensch*. Then, he points to me and says, *klein* mensch. We're outside and standing on dirt. He's facing me, takes a step back, and draws squiggly lines between us with his fingers in the dirt. He makes motions like waves, takes a cup of water that someone next to him had, and pours it on the squiggly lines. He says *Fluss*, and I'm pretty sure he meant water or a river. Then he grabs my arm and pulls me across the drawing next to him. Pointing at me with his right index finger, he says, *zuerst*. Which sounds a lot like first."

"And you think that means what?"

Markus closed his eyes and tilted his head to the left. "I think he said that *klein mensch*, like me—Homo sapien, live across the water or river. And I'm the first ever to cross the river and come to their village."

"So you're saying that there are other humans here inside the Earth? Across the river. The river by the Intruder where we landed?"

"I can't know for sure, but maybe," Markus said.

"Is that all?"

"Well," Markus said and bit his lower lip. "He introduced me to this...woman. Young woman. I gathered it was his daughter. He grabbed my hand and placed it on her hand. He kept saying, *Beitreten. Beitreten.*"

"So he wants you to take his daughter," Jared said. "Probably to marry and make babies. I have to admit, that's a boss move to evolve his species. What would you give her on a scale from one to ten?"

"Probably a six—"

"That's not too bad," Jared said.

"You didn't let me finish," Markus said. "A six after a twelve pack of beers...and if she shaved."

"Okay, I think we've wasted enough time. Let's go see Big Daddy out there and play Let's Make a Deal," Jared said, stepping toward the opening and coming out on the other side.

Hammer and Rat stood like saints with holy powers. A line of Neanderthals lined up by each, waiting to take a turn touching their uniforms. Rat had his sleeves rolled up, and the ladies took a particular interest in his tattoos.

The leader had a young woman standing next to him. Like the other Neanderthals, her cheeks were fuller than a human's. Her nose looked too large for her face and was noticeably broader. Lips were plump, but Jared saw no five o'clock shadow from that distance. "Coyote woman," he said to himself.

"Where's—" Hammer started and stopped when Markus joined Jared in front of the teepee.

"Markus!" Rat shouted. "How's it hanging?"

"Lower than yours!" Markus said, obvious delight in his voice to be rejoined with his teammates.

"Y'all can stop healing the blind and raising the dead," Jared said. "Let's make Big Daddy an offer he can't refuse."

Rat and Hammer raised their hands and motioned for the crowd to move back.

The leader barked an order, and they complied.

Jared keyed in his radio, "You following, Gear?"

"Yep. Been here the whole time. Welcome back, Markus," Gear said.

"*Muchas gracias, amigo*," Markus said, loud enough for the radio to pick up.

"Tell the leader thank you for taking care of our friend and that we're leaving," Jared said.

Danken Sie für taking Pflege von unser Freund. Wir werden Sein going.

The chief puffed out his big lips even larger and shook his head. He put one hand over the other and said, "*Beitreten*."

Join, the radio translated.

"Tell him we will trade four uniforms for Markus and us to leave now."

"I'm not walking back naked through the jungle," Rat said. "Those dinosaurs might think it's bait dangling between my legs."

"I've seen you naked. I think you're safe," Jared said. "We'll let a few of them follow us back to the Intruder and give them an old set. They can even have my dirty underwear."

Im exchage für unser departure jetzt, wir werden geben Sie vier uniforms.

The chief once again shook his head. "*Beitreten*."

The young woman kept her gaze on the ground, looking like she would rather be anywhere else.

"Big Daddy thinks highly of his Princess Fiona," Jared said. "Ask him what his price is for us to leave."

Was ist Ihre price für uns nach verlassen?

"*Nein price. Herausforderung!*" the chief said.

"No price. Even I understand that," Jared said. "I hope *her-rouse-ford-rung* doesn't mean blowjob."

No price. Challenge! the radio translated.

"Challenge?" Jared said. "What kind of challenge?"

Was Art von Herausforderung?

A head floated above the crowd and pushed his way to the forefront.

The chief's daughter looked up and glowed as if she saw her savior. "*Brax!*" she shouted and ran to him.

The chief grabbed her by the arm and held her back. "*Herausforderung! Markus sollen defeat Brax im Auftrag nach Unterbrechung das joining.*

Markus must defeat Brax to break the joining, the radio translated.

"F' that," Markus said.

"Ain't no way Markus can beat that sasquatch!" Jared said.

"We have a better chance shooting our way out of this," Hammer said.

"Yeah, but the results would be all of us dead instead of just Markus," Jared said.

"Hey, you're not giving up Markus to save our butts, are you?" Rat asked.

"Of course not," Jared said. "Gear, tell the chief Markus is sick from the meat he ate. Someone has to fight in his place."

Markus ist ill von eating schlecht Lebensmittel. Jemand sonst werden nehmen seine Ort.

"Jared! You're the captain, but there is no way you can beat that guy," Markus said. "I can't let you take a beating meant for me."

The chief and a few of his counsel spoke in a hush. Turning, the chief said, "*Ich werden Lassen Sie pflücken ein champion.*"

I will let you pick a champion, the radio translated.

"I agree, Markus. That oaf would bust me up in no time," Jared said. "Rat, looks like it's your time in the sun."

"ME?" Rat asked. "Why me?"

Jared approached the gym rat and said, "Because your muscles have muscles. He might be bigger than you, but you're faster. You have a few MMA fights under your belt. I'm counting on your brute strength, but more on your brains, to beat that guy."

"Brains?" Rat said. "You're counting on my brains?" He cleared his throat and wiped a small tear forming in his left eye. "Why, that's the nicest thing you've ever told me."

"I mean it," Jared said. "You're good enough. You're smart enough, and doggone it, people like you. Now, get ready to rumble. You got this!" He took Rat's rifle and walked with him by the chief.

Rat shed his backpack and helmet and stripped off his shirt. The natives audibly marveled at his newly exposed tatted chest and back.

One of the chief's counsel pointed to the knife on Rat's side, which the petty officer removed from the sheath and handed to Jared. He then turned to Brax, whose body swayed side to side, reminding Jared of a scene from the Planet of the Apes.

"*Geben Sie Zimmer. Challange!*" the chief yelled.

The crowd backed away, forming an open circle about twenty feet wide. Cheers and jeers electrified the air.

Brax shook his fists to the sky and yelled.

Rat stepped backward and put some distance between him and his opponent. He kept his feet moving and shifted his shoulders from one side to the other. With fists up, he waited as Brax approached.

The Neanderthal took the first swing. His right fist flew from his side and missed Rat's face by over a foot. Undeterred, he threw the same punch again and returned with the same results.

"You got 'em, Rat," Jared yelled. "Wear his ass out."

Brax pretended to throw the same punch once again but suddenly switched to his left fist and let one fly.

Using his height to his advantage, Rat ducked and delivered a smashing blow dead center to the solar plexus.

Shock contorted Brax's face, and he let out a groan that would have scared a T. rex.

Rat danced away, but as Brax brought his hands to his stomach, the soldier stepped to the side and brought an elbow to the giant's right kidney.

The Neanderthal spun around, and the back of his right arm knocked Rat face-first to the ground.

The crowd roared in victory, and for the first time, Jared felt like these civilized sub-humans could turn into animals at the smell of blood.

Brax yelled, clasped both hands above his head, and dropped to the ground, sending a crushing blow.

The muscleman had enough intuition to roll over and get back on his feet as quickly as possible, missing the hit by a microsecond. With Brax on his knees, he bounded over, looped his right arm underneath his opponent's neck, and secured a headlock. His left hand pushed down on the head. He then wrapped his legs around Brax's torso—completing a bare naked choke hold. With adrenaline pumping, his body shook as he strained to stop the air and blood supply.

Thrashing about, Brax tried to pull Rat's arm from around his neck without success. He gasped and grunted, then threw himself back first to the ground.

The fall jolted Rat, but he maintained his hold—dogging Brax's fingers as they desperately tried to grab hair or an ear. His teeth clenched tightly. Veins on his arms and forehead bulged. Spit foamed at the corner of his mouth. He yelled in rage as he redoubled his efforts.

Then, the massive body of Brax went limp. It was as if someone had thrown a switch.

The chief cast a disgusted gaze toward the fallen warrior. His face contorted as if he had smelled a rotting dinosaur.

Princess Fiona ran and started hitting Rat as he released his grip and pulled himself from under Brax's dead weight.

"Hey! Stop!" Rat protested and raised his left arm to deflect the blows. "He's not dead. Brax will wake up in a few minutes." He turned to his crew and hurried to be by their side. "Jared, tell them he isn't dead."

"I'm on it," Gear said.

Brax ist nicht tot. Er ist gerade schlafend. Er werden aufwachen bald.

Fiona laid her head on Brax's chest. She rose and fell with each deep breath he took. "*Er's am Leben.*"

The crowd let out a sigh of relief. Then, they clapped in a rhythm that must have indicated something specific.

"Are they clapping for me or that Brax is still alive?" Rat said.

"They're all looking at you," Jared said. "You've got a fan base."

Rat raised a fist in victory and bowed before putting on his shirt.

"Nice job, Rat," Markus said. "But I think I could have taken him."

"Yeah? Maybe taken him to lunch," Rat said while securing his buttons.

"I think it's time we leave on a high note," Hammer said. "Jared, don't let these guys jerk you around."

"Don't worry. I'll put on my poker face. But I won't be bluffin' with my muffin," Jared said.

Hammer closed his eyes and dropped his head. "Keep it serious…please, Captain?"

"Stand tall, everyone. It's showtime!" Jared said, leading his team to the chief.

"Gear, tell the chief we have met the challenge and are leaving now."

Wir haben getroffen das Herausforderung und dass wir sind leaving jetzt.

The chief showed no emotion and locked gazes with Jared. The seconds ticked by. Jared returned the same deadpan look and consciously chose not to blink. After what seemed like an eternity, the chief turned to his entourage and spoke too low for the radio to pick up and translate.

"I'm not liking this," Hammer said. "Everyone get ready. If they try something, shoot the closest or the ones with weapons. I'll start by eliminating the chief. If we drop enough of them, they may scatter."

"Everyone, give Hammer your knives," Jared said, pulling his out and handing it over. "Hammer, give me your cigar lighter."

"My cigar lighter?" Hammer said.

"Come on, gimme. You go nowhere without it. We're going to offer parting gifts," Jared said.

Begrudgingly, the weapon specialist reached into his pocket and gave the lighter to Jared. "That's the best lighter I ever had."

The chief turned to face the humans.

"Hammer, give them the knives," Jared said.

The soldier did as he was told, careful to offer handles first. Eager hands reached out and took them.

Jared had the lighter in his right hand, ready to go. "Hey, Chief. Get a load of this." He flicked the spark wheel, and a blue flame popped up. "See…fire."

The Neanderthals weren't afraid but were highly interested. One of the chief's men stepped forward and slowly reached toward the flame.

"Fire…hot…hot," Jared said.

The subhuman stuck a finger out, briefly touched the flame, and retracted. Then he tried again, letting the finger close enough to get hot. He instinctively jerked his hand back and put his burnt finger in his mouth.

"Yeah, baby…fire," Jared said. He reached to the ground, plucked some of the scrubby grass, and held it to the flame. "See, it burns."

The crowd close enough to see made sounds of wonderment.

Jared closed the lid on the lighter and approached the chief. He then pulled the lid back and slowly operated the spark wheel, which kicked off sparks. With his other hand, he pushed the fuel button, and the flame shot up. He removed his finger from the fuel button and demonstrated how he could move the wheel with his thumb and bring it to rest on the fuel button. "You got it? Here, try it."

The chief pursed his lips and created a few sparks. One attempt was successful, and the flame lasted about a second.

"You gotta hold the button down if you want flame," Jared said, reaching for and pushing the fuel button.

On the next try, the chief mastered the device. He poked his chest out and raised the lighter high, turning and showing the adoring subjects that he had become the fire king.

"Okay, guys. This is where we exit the stage left," Jared said. "We're going to double-time it back to the Intruder, and we don't let anything slow us down."

CHAPTER 13

No walls protected the city, but large columns sparsely fronted the perimeter. A massive archway in the center was wide enough for ten T-90m tanks to enter three meters apart.

Kolya noticed there were no checkpoints or armed personnel out front. Anyone, or anything, could enter without hindrance. In a land of prehistoric giants, the situation defied logic.

The soft beat of drums and the coo of flutes greeted them several meters before walking under the arch. It felt reassuring to be part of civilization once again. Kolya turned to Misha and saw a smile on the young man's face from ear to ear.

"The arch is made of perfectly carved stones," Misha said.

Kolya was close enough to see no mortar lines. These stones were cut so precisely that they fit practically seamlessly. The various hieroglyphics of birds, animals, and men appeared as if they had been cast in a mold.

The ground gave way to a hard, smooth surface, making the wide paths, or roads, that crisscrossed, from what he could see, of the city. The main pathway they were on was the widest of all other offshoots. Tall poles on either side had purple-colored tarps stretched across, each about seven meters long, offering shade for those who traveled the path.

Several children kicked a ball made of hide and ran in front of them, quickly disappearing down the adjacent pathway.

Four men hustled over, pushing what looked like a coffin. The men wore single-piece garments of bleached animal hide covering their chests and mid-thigh. They gingerly removed the dead warrior from the pole and carefully laid him in the wooden box.

The men bowed and hurried off while Gamba moved the group forward.

Large buildings lined the road, with people teeming in front. Some strode about as if on a casual walk. Others sat at tables while eating and drinking. Palm-like trees decorated the area. Vendors with various wares waved and invited buyers to visit. The heavenly smell of cooking meat wafted from an outside grill.

All the people turned and bowed briefly as Gamba led the entourage. This told Kolya that the young man was more than just an ordinary member of this society. He looked too young to be a leader, but then he remembered that King Tutankhamun rose to power at an early age.

Oddly, as the group passed, the people stopped what they were doing and started following.

There were several 'vehicles' defying gravity along the road. Some were wheelless carts filled with unique items pushed effortlessly by their owners. Two men guided a three-by-nine-meter structure loaded with large blocks of stone that must have weighed tons! They pushed it along and chatted casually as if it was not there. At least three people, old and perhaps too infirm to walk, sat in elevated chairs next to someone who guided them with one hand on the back of the chair. People rode in vehicles similar to rickshaws and pulled by a single person. These moved to the side and stopped to let Gamba pass.

"I have not seen a wheel. Can a race this advanced not have invented the wheel?" Misha asked.

"Perhaps there was no need for a wheel," Kolya said. "When you have mastered gravity, the wheel no longer serves its most useful purpose."

"And I do not see any animals," Misha said. "There are images of animals everywhere. The people could use animals to pull the floating carts and such."

"The other side of the city has few stone structures and large green areas. That side—near the river—could be used for keeping animals. The advantage of not using animals for transportation is you do not have to clean up after them."

Dima approached Kolya and said, "Vanya is not doing well."

The fascination of the city had drawn his attention from his injured comrade. He looked and saw the older soldier taking each step robotically. His face had lost color and was contorted with pain.

"If we do not stop soon, I will request to rest," Kolya said.

The main road ended at the giant pyramid in the city's center. Vanya could not make it that far. A short distance away, an opulent palace came into view. Kolya moved over to Gamba's side, pointed toward it, and nodded.

Gamba returned the nod and said, "*A lọ si aafin lati pade baba mi.*"

Unable to understand, Kolya had to believe the response was an acknowledgment of their destination. He went to Vanya's side and said, "Put your arm around me. I will help you walk. We only have to make it to the palace."

Vanya lifted his gaze from the ground, looked to the left, and then at Kolya. "I can make it on my own." He stiffened his back and walked with more assured steps.

Sensing that his presence only agitated the situation, Kolya returned to Dima's side. "The man has the demeanor of a wounded dog. Willing to bite the hand that feeds it."

Dima shrugged his shoulders. "Eh, he is gruff when scared."

Stunned, Kolya said, "Vanya...afraid? I have never seen the man back away from any situation—no matter the odds."

"His inner fear stokes his anger," Dima said. "He is quiet when he is confident."

Vanya was a man of few words who kept his interactions with his comrades to a minimum, regardless of the situation. The hardened front seemed to drop only after a half bottle of Stolichnaya was in his belly.

Each step brought them closer to the palace, divided into two fifty-meter sections by an ornate copper picket gate ten meters wide on the first floor and seven meters tall. Various hieroglyphs and colorful images of people covered the front of the buildings. Two men with tall spears guarded the gates. The second story stood taller than the first, perhaps twelve meters, but each side wasn't as broad. In fact, the second story extended to the rear of the palace, leaving an open area behind the gate that Kolya believed would serve as a courtyard. Images of animals and people fronted the second story.

Several steps led up to the gate. Kolya looked behind as they reached the top and saw at least three hundred people had followed. The guards looked forward but showed no emotion as they approached.

"It is so beautiful," Misha said, his eyes wide.

"In a quiet lagoon, devils dwell," Vanya muttered, then spat.

The guards slid each gate open parallel with the front. Kolya noticed the black material with the goldish glow on each end of the pickets.

The reddish-brown floor gave way to white stone, polished to the point Kolya felt out of place walking on it with his boots. Bringing in the dead carcass of a dinosaur felt like a greater sin.

Kolya estimated the courtyard to be ten meters wide and fifty meters deep. In the center, a rectangular pool had a three-meter-tall obelisk made of pale greenish stone spilling water from four openings near the top into large white bowls on pedestals higher than the pool water.

Seven-meter-tall square columns supported one side of second-floor structures, with intricate burnt orange and turquoise blue stones forming long and thin patterns.

Between the columns sat three meters wide and one-meter-tall pots containing various blooming flowers that gave off sweet scents of honey and vanilla.

The second story had rugs hanging over sections of the outside, some rolled up, revealing they were covers for open windows.

As they rounded the fountain, two figures sat on decorated chairs on a pedestal nine meters wide, with stone posts supporting a canopy. A guard stood to either side, holding copper-colored swords with half-moon blades.

Over on the right side, an area with burning candles resembled a shrine.

The man wore a black stone forehead headband. Striped animal hide covered his shoulders and draped just under his neck, leaving his chest bare. Animal hide of a dark solid color covered his loins, leaving his legs bare to his sandals.

The woman's long, silk-looking dress reached the floor. The top and sash across her waist were white. Half of the lower part of the dress was purple, the same color as the tarpaulins shading the entrance road. The other half was white. She wore a purple cape that hung to the floor.

Gamba brought the group to a halt a few meters before the royalty. He bowed and dropped to one knee, as did the other warriors.

Kolya looked at his team and saw no one felt compelled to follow. He did not know if it was the right or wrong thing to do, but he had no intention of getting on a knee for any man.

Rising, as did his warriors, Gamba approached the king and queen on the thrones, who rose and greeted him with hugs and kisses.

The three spoke for several minutes. Gamba obviously recanted the adventure of the hunt, sometimes pointing to Kolya and his comrades. The king's face often showed confusion, and Gamba elaborated with hand gestures and made sounds of firearms.

The queen just listened and wore a perpetual smile. She either understood or didn't care about the story being told.

The king pointed to the carcass and said something.

Gamba pointed with palms turned upward at the dead animal.

With that, the king lifted his right thumb.

One warrior took his knife and cut a portion of the dead meat. He then took it to Gamba, who brought it to the shrine and placed it on top of a rectangular stone box about three meters wide and one meter deep.

Gamba picked up a candle and brought the flame low into the box. Flames whooshed up, and a blazing fire crackled throughout the box. Black smoke billowed upward.

A warrior brought Gamba another piece from the hunt, and he put that on the fire, too.

As the smoke rose, shouts emerged from the populace gathered outside.

The king turned his gaze toward Kolya and his comrades. He then extended his right arm and poked up his thumb, which he turned and pointed to the floor.

Kolya let his rifle slide off his shoulder and grabbed the barrel with his left hand—bringing his right hand onto the stock and holding it across his body. He was determined he and his men would not be burnt offerings to the god of this world.

CHAPTER 14

The hoard of Neanderthals didn't bother to pursue Jared and his men as they dashed away from the village. Six of the sentries at the checkpoints attempted to block their escape but succumbed to the non-lethal sedative pellets from their pistols.

Jared was concerned that the Neanderthals knew the location of the Intruder. It would only be a matter of time before the subhumans visited again, and the fuel in the lighter would run out soon enough. They only had so many uniforms and sundries to trade to appease them. There were enough cavemen to make Jared and his crew prisoners inside the Intruder. The last thing he wanted to do was kill them. But when the rescue plane showed up, he might have a tough choice to make.

"Start heading about ten degrees to your left," Gear said over the radio.

They were back in the woods, slowed down by the ground clutter and towering trees. The animal life significantly increased the deeper they traveled. Jared kept telling himself to watch for danger, but his mind kept racing toward a quick sponge bath, something to eat—even an MRE sounded good—and some much-needed rest. Something about this place increased his appetite and wore him down faster than topside.

"The woods are thinning again," Rat said, who was about ten feet in the lead. Hammer brought up the backside with Markus in lockstep. "We'll be exposed for a while."

"You're a good hour away," Gear said. "Godspeed."

Jared couldn't put his finger on it, but it seemed as if they had been humping it for half a day and should have been a lot closer to home. This place had a strange effect on reality.

A dinosaur burst through the foliage between two trees. It topped over ten feet and stood on two legs. The neck looked unusually long for a biped. Its snake-like head had an evil smile. Jared imagined that's what a demon from Hell would look like. This beastie had an array of blue feathers running from the top of its head and down its spine to the short tail. Its body feathers were the color of a robin's breast, with a hint of blue feathers mixed in.

Jared didn't have time to utter a curse when the Therizinosaurus reached out an oversized hand with three-foot-long claws and cut through the air—missing him by a hair's width.

Panicked, he squeezed the trigger on the JNY-7, shooting bursts straight up without aim.

The rifle's discharge confused the dinosaur so that it retreated a few steps backward.

"Where is it?" Rat called out.

Hammer quickly joined Jared by his side. Weaponless, Markus took cover behind the two.

"It's over there—behind that tree," Hammer said. He fired a three-burst, peppering the tree trunk.

The dinosaur roared angrily and ran. It stepped back into view as it reached Rat, snaking its head forward to put the bite on its prey.

Rat jumped back and yelled—catching his foot on a root and falling on his side.

Hammer fired first, then Jared joined in, placing the explosive bullets in the dinosaur's chest.

Meat exploded—sending flesh and blood everywhere. The Therizinosaurus wobbled before collapsing as dead weight.

"Yuck," Rat said. He rose and wiped the gore off his face with his hands. "I need a towel." Looking around, he saw a bush with large leaves and wiped his hands on them. "Like taking a ground meat shower."

"You're welcome," Jared said.

"Hey, I'm glad you got it before it got me. I'm just sayin'," Rat said.

Markus poked around at the dead dinosaur with a stick he had picked up. "The claws on this thing are unbelievable. They're as long as my arm."

"Yeah, that thing would give Freddy Krueger nightmares," Jared said. "Why is it I'm the one that dino attacks first? This is the second time."

"Maybe it's your Polo Black cologne," Markus said.

"I don't think bold notes of iced mango, silver armoise, and sandalwood make me today's special," Jared said.

"You know the laws of nature," Hammer said, while trying to repress a smile. "The predator picks out the weakest of the flock. Being the smallest of stature, I think it's obvious you look the least intimidating."

Jared's head dropped like a wilted flower. "Et tu, Hammer?" His eyes closed, and he bit his lip.

Concerned, Hammer said, "Hey, man. I was funning with you. Come on!"

"I'm over it," Jared said, returning to life like a Pop-Tart springing from a toaster. "Let's get going before the all-you-can-eat dead dinosaur buffet begins."

"I see everyone's okay," Gear said. "I just got an update from Command. The rescue plane will arrive shortly."

"What?" Jared exclaimed. "You mean we're finally getting out of here?" He turned and gave his crew a high five. "That's such good news. I'll put bad Jared on the shelf and let good Jared come out of prison."

"Good Jared?" Rat said. "I don't think I ever met him. Is he going to apologize for everything bad Jared said to me?"

"Don't push it, meathead," Jared said. "Wait—I take it back. My bad. Don't push it, Mister Micheli, sir."

"That's better," Rat said.

"Guys, let's get out of here," Hammer said. Sweat dripped down his ruddy cheeks onto his chin.

"If we come across anything that moves, shoot it," Jared said.

Rat led the way as if he were running a race. The open area quickly gave way to more woods, and none of the dinosaurs in the distance had given them a second look. As instructed, the young man took shots into the brush, and he paved the way.

Jared almost told the boy he didn't literally mean to shoot anything that moves but decided that no harm would come of it. It might prove fantastic advice.

Time ticked by. Eventually, Gear said over the radio, "You guys are about to clear the woods. You'll be minutes from home."

"I see it! I see the Intruder," Rat yelled.

Rat was the first out of the forest, then Hammer, Markus, and Jared.

"Guys, if you look up, you'll see something that should make you very happy," Gear announced.

The rescue aircraft was there! Another Intruder descended without the slightest bit of sound, and pterosaurs took to the skies from the treetops and flew toward it.

"I hope those lizard birds don't muck up this mission," Jared said.

A buzz sounded overhead, and two of the nearest flying reptiles exploded into a mist.

"I guess I was worried about nothing," Jared said.

Gear exited the Intruder and watched the rescue plane slowly descend.

Jared and his crew ran toward it like they were running a track event.

The rescue Intruder set out its landing gear and rested gently on the ground. The escape door opened. Out stepped a tall man in need of a shave. He wore a brown fedora, leather jacket, khaki pants, and shirt. A Colt .45 was on his side.

"*Comment ça va?*" the man said.

"I know this guy from back home. He's a local celebrity. Erik Lott." Jared turned his gaze to Hammer. "We're inside the Earth, with dinosaurs and Neanderthals. And Command sends a Cajun Indiana Jones to save us. This story can't get any weirder."

CHAPTER 15

Two guards and Gamba led Kolya and his comrades to double doors on the palace's first floor. The guards pulled the doors open, and Gamba stepped into the room.

Kolya held his rifle closely against his chest, trying to be non-threatening but ready for the unexpected. He looked back at the others and nodded. They, too, were prepared to act if threatened—even Vanya.

Gamba waited for them to file in. He smiled, waved his right hand away from his side, and said, "*O you ri awọn abuse lati wa ni ita. O le wẹ labẹ omi Combahee. Ounje ati ohun mimu yoo de laipẹ.*" Then he left, and the doors closed behind him.

The room was seven meters wide and nearly fifteen meters long. Ten beds lined one side, and three tables and chairs were on the opposite side. The ceiling was five meters high, and the walls had no windows. The side of the room with the beds was in shadowed darkness. Light shone on the tables and chairs from openings in the ceiling. At the end of the room, water poured from a copper pipe onto the floor, surrounded by drains.

One table had animal skins fashioned into clothing the natives wore. A stack of folded cloths was set next to two palm-sized rectangular objects.

Kolya noticed when he stepped in that the room temperature felt cooler. The splashing water from the shower had a soothing effect—at least, he thought.

"After the king made the gesture of thumbs down, this is the last gift I had expected to come," Dima said as he set down his bag.

"I, too, thought we might fight our last battle," Kolya said. "It is good we did not overreact. There is much to be learned about their customs and ways."

"This place is nice," Misha said as he walked over to a table and set down a duffle bag. "Clean clothing." He picked up a loincloth and felt it. "It's softer than I thought it would be." His fingers gently caressed the cloths and picked up the rectangular object, giving it a sniff. "The towels feel like cotton. And this is soap." He then looked over at the wall and stepped over by it. "Vents in the floor," he reached down and hovered an open palm above it. "Cool air is coming from here."

Vanya took a seat at a nearby table. The table and chairs were made of wood, but the chair seats were made of woven material. The soldier closed his eyes and looked relieved.

Dima reached down to one bed and felt the mattress. "Feels comfortable enough." He picked up the blanket covering the bed and smelled it. "It's clean—even has a sweet scent like perfume."

"It might be lavender," Misha said. "Lavender can help you sleep."

"Yes, sleep," Vanya said wistfully. "We lay our heads down to sleep—dreaming of the bounties of our Motherland. We sleep…and we never wake again."

The doors opened. Kolya spun around with his rifle, pointing at the two girls who entered.

They were young—perhaps early teens. Both had dark, coarse hair with bangs across their foreheads and the sides hanging straight down. Their bronze skin tones showcased their lips, which were deep dark purple. Each carried a large wooden tray loaded with fruits, cheeses, and meats. A single garment covered their bodies to mid-thigh. They soundlessly stepped over to an empty table and placed the trays down.

Another younger girl walked in with a tray holding a pitcher and four cups, which she placed in front of Vanya.

The three bowed together before skipping out the door and giggling. The doors closed behind them.

"Food!" Misha said with much delight.

The three men standing hurried to the table and examined the offering.

"Yes, eat," Vanya said. "It is what they want you to do."

Misha and Dima turned their gazes on Kolya.

After expelling a lungful of air, Kolya said, "The people here have had many opportunities to kill us. I do not believe they would have spent the energy to poison this food if they had wanted us dead. I, for one, will take my chances and eat it." He picked out a plum from one platter and took a bite. After a few chews, he said, "It is delicious."

Misha grabbed a piece of meat and chomped it down. "Do you think this is from the kill? Are we eating food sacrificed to their god or gods?"

"I do not think so," Kolya said. "That meat cooked to the point of catching on fire." He went to Vanya's table, picked up the pitcher, and filled a cup. The liquid was red and smelled slightly of ethanol mixed with fruit. He tasted it and said, "They have given us wine. We must limit the amount that we enjoy." Pouring another cup, he slid it over in front of Vanya.

He eyed the cup for several seconds and then picked up the cup and gulped a mouthful. "If you wake up and you are not in pain, then you know you are dead."

Vanya's words made him laugh. "Then, while you are living, find time to enjoy the flowers while they bloom." He handed an apple to him and filled the other two cups.

The men ate and drank their fill. Grapes, apples, plums, and oranges—little difference from what was in their world. The meat was tender, not overcooked, and seasoned with an unusual but not unpleasant spice. One cheese reminded him of *Rossiysky*.

Afterward, each took a turn in the shower. Kolya was surprised to feel heated water in the shower—indeed, nothing that warm could have come straight from the ground or even the river. The water had no smell or taste, not unlike bottled water. He and his comrades washed their uniforms and underwear while in the shower and draped them across the backs of chairs and over the vents, blowing cool air to dry them. Inside the room, the loincloths were suitable enough for wear.

Dima volunteered for the first watch, which turned into a demand. Kolya had insisted he would be the first but stopped short of giving the man an order.

Vanya was the first to lie down. Misha helped him pull the thin covers to his chin. He was snoring only moments after his head hit the flat pillow.

Kolya waited for Misha to get into bed before he checked to see if Dima had changed his mind. Nothing had changed as he imagined. The mattress was a third of a meter thick. It had some cushiony effect but was nothing like a modern mattress. Still, it was more comfortable than sleeping on a stone floor. He closed his eyes, and even though he was beyond tired, it felt like sleeping would be impossible.

Kolya woke with a start when something fell across his legs. It was Dima, but his vision went in and out of focus before he could help the man back up. He felt incredibly heavy. As he looked at the light hitting the tables and chairs, he saw a mist emanating from the vents in the floor. His mouth opened, but he could not find his voice. The world slowly faded to dark.

CHAPTER 16

"Indiana Jones, eh," Lott said. "I bet your mama put tomatoes in her gumbo."

"My mama was Creole," Jared said. "So, yeah. She did. I bet you put Kitchen Bouquet in your jambalaya to make it brown."

Lott passed his gaze over Jared and his crew. "Lieutenant Commander Erik Lott, here. Sent by General Mitchell to pull your butts out of a most unexpected circumstance." He looked at Jared and said, "My jambalaya is brown because of my cooking technique of creating the perfect dark roux. Far superior to the Creole version, which reminds me of a rice and tomato stew."

"I'd appreciate it if you two Louisiana rivals could redirect your attention back to the mission," Gear said. "I'm Petty Officer First Class Michael Babin. You can call me 'Gear.' And if you want to settle your differences with a cookoff, I will gladly judge."

"Don't tempt him. Cajuns will eat anything that moves. He'd serve up a T. rex étouffée in a heartbeat," Jared said.

"I didn't bring any rice," Lott said. "But if an opportunity arises, and if it's anything like an alligator, I could fry up some Tyrannosaurus tail meat."

"I'd eat it," Rat said. "Petty Officer First Class Sam Micheli. Call me 'Rat.'"

"Or Rat bastard," Jared said.

"Hey! You said you wouldn't call me that anymore," Rat protested.

"Lieutenant Commander Jared Belazaire," Jared said. "I don't care what you call me. Just don't call me for dinner."

"Special Warfare Operator Petty Officer First Class Bret Handcock. Call me 'Hammer.'"

"Markus Daniel, First Class Petty Officer. Markus is just fine. When I'm not being dragged through jungles by

Neanderthals and running from dinosaurs, I pilot the Intruder."

"Yes, General Mitchell gave me the report on indigenous wildlife and hominin. It's quite fascinating. I would have never believed it, but I saw some real-time videos of your close encounters," Lott said.

"I transmitted the videos to Lieutenant Lott during his trip," Gear said.

"I'm surprised how Command could get you here so quickly," Jared said. "Not that I'm complaining."

"Uh, his arrival didn't come as quick as you think," Gear said.

"Right. You went missing five days ago," Lott said. "It took Command a couple of days to decide a plan of action and a few more to get me and my equipment over the North Pole."

"I know there is no night and day here. But my watch tells me we've been here less than a day," Jared said.

"Time passes quicker on the outside," Gear said. "We can communicate in real-time with quantum communications, but an hour inside the Earth is much slower than out."

"Potato, po-tot-oe," Jared said. "Let's just get the F' out of here."

"Well," Lott lifted his fedora and brushed back his short, blond hair, "we can't leave until we complete the mission."

"The mission was to get Element One-Fifteen back to Area Fifty-One. Flapping our lips down here ain't getting us there any faster," Jared said.

"Command sees the unexpected turn of events as an opportunity," Lott said. "An opportunity to retrieve DNA samples from the dinosaurs. As many as practically possible."

"Wait, what?" Jared asked.

"The mission has expanded to include gathering dinosaur DNA. I have sample kits in my aircraft. The length of the mission will be at my discretion," Lott said. "How long we stay depends on the number of samples and the difficulty of acquiring them."

"We can kill them as fast as you can line them up," Jared said. "My men and I are too tired to play Duck Hunt right now. We'll have to get some shuteye before getting any Jurassic Park seeds."

"What about the Neanderthals?" Markus asked. "There're over a thousand of them, and they know our location. That many people could damage our escape aircraft."

"You saw how the guns on the Intruder made the threat from the pterosaurs disappear," Lott said. "I recommend you move anything of value into the rescue plane as soon as possible."

"You mean kill them? They're just people, and this is their world. We're the bad guys here. What about the Prime Directive?"

"Markus, we ain't playing Star Track," Jared said.

"Star Trek."

"Star Wars, Star Trek, Starbucks—it don't matter," Jared said. "We take our orders from Command. If they say we have to take out Fred Flintstone and his merry men, we do it."

"Markus, I'm not in the business of killing innocent men. I'd like nothing better than capturing a Neanderthal and returning him home to study. But Command has forbidden me of that. This may be our only chance to get prehistoric genetic material," Lott said. "We're the good guys. We'll always be the good guys. Never question that."

Markus turned his gaze to Jared, who brought his index finger to his lips and shook his head.

"Gentlemen, the sooner you rest, the sooner we leave," Lott said. "I brought my accordion if you'd like to be serenaded by a little Cajun music."

"I'd have to be blind drunk on a bottle of peach Crown Royal to listen to chank-a-chank music," Jared said. "But one thing I'd like to know."

"What's that?" Lott asked.

"What is that thing around your neck?" Jared said. "That beetle-looking thing is glowing."

"Glowing?" Lott said. "It's a piece of jewelry—a scarab from ancient Egypt. I found it on a dig, and the Egyptian Government gave it to me as a gift. It's made of black sardonyx, I believe, but it doesn't glow."

"Take it off and look at it," Jared said.

Lott reached behind his head and fumbled with the leather choker. Once unfastened, he brought it around for inspection.

"Wha—" He turned his head from side to side and pursed his lips. After rubbing his eyes and refocusing, he said, "Uh, I have no explanation. I've never seen it glow like this before."

"Can I see it?" Gear asked.

"Sure," Lott said. He dropped the choker about a foot above Gear's open palm. The amulet remained suspended in the air while the leather hung down.

"Look at that!" Rat said. "It's floating."

Lott snatched the choker and examined the amulet. He then opened his hand and let it hang in the air. Taking a finger, he moved the amulet downward for a few seconds before moving it back upward. "I don't know what to make of this. It's uncanny."

"We must ask ourselves, what's different about the Underworld for it to act that way?" Gear said. "It's not the dinosaurs. It may have something to do with the substitute sun up there. We don't know what it's made of or just what it is. But so far, we have witnessed no other overt anomaly. However, Element One-Fifteen brought us here and is only fifty feet away inside the Intruder. Perhaps that is giving the amulet unique characteristics."

"I'd like to have a look at the element," Lott said.

"Ain't much to see," Jared said. "Follow me." Jared headed for the Intruder, and Lott joined him by his side.

Each member climbed the steep steps into the aircraft. Once inside, Gear raised the steps, sealing the bottom of the Intruder.

Jared headed straight to his locker, hung up his rifle, and let the backpack slide off his shoulders onto the floor. "Gear, show Lieutenant Commander Lott the magic ball from Goofy Golf."

"You can drop the Lieutenant Commander formality," Lott said. "Erik will suffice."

"You don't speak like any Cajun I've met," Rat said as he put away his gear. "Too sophisticated."

"I keep my education and culture separate," Erik said. "Although after an afternoon of pinching tails and sucking heads, the beer degrades my vocabulary quite a bit."

"Pinching tails and sucking heads," Hammer said. "I'm afraid to ask what that means."

"He's talking about eating crawfish," Jared said. "The fastest way to get the meat out of a crawfish tail is to pinch the bottom of the tail while pulling the meat out with your teeth. Some people suck the heads to get a hit of spicy crawfish boil water and the yellow fat inside."

"Oh. I've spent most of my life in Florida," Hammer said. "I love a good seafood boil. There isn't anything inside a lobster head I'd want to eat."

"The element is over here," Gear said while approaching the table. "In this bismuth box."

"Bismuth? Why bismuth?" Erik asked and peered down into the box.

"Command didn't say why," Gear said. "It was in the box when we traveled over the North Pole, so I don't think the bismuth shields any of its properties."

"Shield its properties…Gear, you've given me an idea," Erik said. "This aircraft has an EMF scanner, correct?" Erik asked.

"Yeah," Marus said as he removed his shirt. "The Electromagnetic Field scanner is part of the defensive array." He put on a fresh shirt and sat at the pilot's console.

"Is there a way we could scan the Element One-Fifteen?" Erik asked.

"Hmm, I think I could link the camera from my electronic pad and send that electromagnetic information to the computer for analysis," Gear said. He retrieved the pad from the console and began typing away. After a couple of minutes, he said, "There. Let's try it."

A video of the element from the pad was downloaded to the computer. Gear read the results and said, "The EMF is super high—in the fifty MeV region."

"Okay," Erik said and removed the choker with the amulet. "Scan this."

"It won't read anything," Gear said. "It's made of stone."

"Humor me."

Gear started the video and waited for the results. He turned his gaze to Erik and said, "Fifty MeV. Just like the element."

"What's the point?" Jared asked.

"There is a connection between the element and the amulet. I'm not sure what it is. But the element may give the amulet the power of antigravity."

"That may also suggest," Gear said, "that the scarab is not made of black sardonyx. It may be as unique as the Element One-Fifteen itself."

"Guys," Markus said. "I've got some news."

"Give it to us," Jared said.

"I'm getting the same E-M reading outside the ship…a few miles across the river. There is another source of One-Fifteen in this Underworld."

CHAPTER 17

Kolya woke, feeling a hard surface underneath. A constant roar of many voices carried through the air. He turned his gaze about and discovered he was in a small room with a door made of copper pickets. It was the equivalent of a jail cell.

It took a few seconds for his eyes to adjust and come into full focus. He moved and flexed his extremities and found himself in a sound physical shape. Where was he? Where were his comrades? Gamba? Why did the warrior betray him?

Lying on the floor did not yield answers. Kolya rose and walked by the closed gate. An item of pottery, with round shoulders and an opening on top, rested on the ground. The only article of clothing on his body was the loincloth he had put on before bedding down.

Some fifty meters away, people sat in four tiers of concentric stands. As he looked around, he realized he was in a stadium. Farther in the distance, he saw the top half of the pyramid that centered the city. A bloody carcass—about the size of a cow—sat in the middle of the dusty stadium ground.

A loud voice echoed over the crowd noise, bringing the roar to a hush. From his right, a bipedal dinosaur stepped out from the double gates. It was gray on its back, legs, and arms, while the underside was light tan. He estimated the height to be four meters and the length nine meters. Small sail-shaped ridges lined the top of its head to halfway down its tail. The head was snake-like, and he saw rows of spiked teeth, even at a distance.

The Allosaurus' legs pumped up and down. Its short arms bounced along with the head to balance the weight carried by three-toed feet. The dinosaur's ability to remain upright amazed Kolya. Each step looked like it would fall on its chest, but the other foot coming down would always lift it back up.

It stopped and sniffed the air. After spotting the carcass, it stepped over and began eating.

The crowd noise intensified to his left. He turned and saw another bipedal dinosaur enter the battlefield. The creature was unmistakably a T. rex. Its head was nearly three times larger than the other. The thighs were beefier, and the tail shorter and thicker. It had the color of sun-faded dark green.

The crowd chanted and jeered. Kolya did not doubt what was to transpire. The T. rex wasted no time powering to the center of the field.

The Allosaurus jerked its head up. A flap of meat hung from its open jaws, dripping blood as it uttered a warning.

Instead of attacking directly, the T. rex circled the opponent, who turned its head from one side to the other as it watched.

The T. rex moved to the opposite side of the bait and attempted to steal a mouthful.

The Allosaurus screamed another warning and snapped its jaws into empty air as the T. rex pulled back.

Weaving its head back and forth like a boxer, the T. rex sidestepped the carcass and missed as it tried to bite the Allosaurus' neck.

Although the T. rex was slightly larger than the Allosaurus, its body's build and head size made it appear superior.

The smaller dinosaur showed agility by retaliating with a sweep of its left claws, raking across the T. rex's neck. Three slashes filled with red blood and spilled down to the earth. The attack forced a hiss out of the injured dinosaur.

In an aggressive move, the Allosaurus dipped low as if going for a leg and then sprang upward, catching the T. rex off guard enough to clamp its jaws on the T. rex's neck.

The T. rex roared—sounding like a foghorn—it thrashed about as the Allosaurus struggled to maintain its hold. While twisting its body, the T. rex eventually brought its thick tail flinging from the side and struck the attacker with enough force to break free of its grip.

Despite being injured, the T. rex showed no sign of backing down. It stretched its neck and tail out straight and roared.

The Allosaurus met the challenge and mirrored the T. rex in a roaring standoff, which gave way to the two dinosaurs pacing each other in a circle.

The T. rex lurched forward and surprised the Allosaurus as it bit down on its neck.

When the Allosaurus' tail came in to sweep as it twisted its body, the T. rex planted its right foot down on it—pinning the tail to the ground.

This time, the Allosaurus cried out in pain and anger, but it was powerless to break free.

The T. rex thrashed its head about, slinging blood flowing down its jaws and around the neck of its victim. As the Allosaurus' resistance waned, the T. rex pushed it over on its side and held the death grip of its jaws until the opponent went limp.

Three men ran into view and stood shoulder-to-shoulder before the T. rex. They each held a shiny aluminum device that protruded about a half-meter in their hands and pointed it at the dinosaur. The dinosaur immediately spun around and lumbered away, stopping to turn its head and hiss. The men advanced and spread out, forcing the T. rex to retreat into a huge double-gated archway carved into the stadium from where it came.

Four men trotted to the dead Allosaurus. Two clamped a black collar around its neck, and two clamped a similar collar on the end of its tail. After that, they lifted the dinosaur from the ground and moved it back through the double gates from which it had entered.

The pottery at Kolya's feet drew his attention, and he lifted it from the ground. Liquid sloshed inside as he brought the opening to his nose. It was not wine. His mouth was dry, so he tasted it. It was as clean as the water in the room. He drank a mouthful, then another, holding it for a few seconds before swallowing. It was refreshing, and he reflected on his situation.

Something from the left abruptly struck the gate of his prison. He jumped back, and two warriors appeared carrying long spears. Another warrior entered the view. He held a half-moon copper sword and what looked like a shield made of the same metal.

The two warriors lowered the tips of their spears, keeping Kolya at bay while the other opened the gate. He tossed the sword and shield to the ground before him.

"*Se ihamora ara re ki o ja fun emi re*," the warrior said, backing away and taking the other two with him out of view.

Kolya didn't understand, but arming him meant only one thing. He would have no choice but to enter the battle.

Chants rose from the populace inside the stadium. It was a single word repeated over and over.

There was no one to give him encouragement, to express his feelings, or to whom he could pass his last words if his life should meet its end. Kolya never felt so alone. How he missed his comrades!

Delaying the inevitable would only make matters worse. He picked up the shield. It weighed more than he thought, but he noticed it was because of the thickness. The curved sword blade felt awkward in his hand. There would be no way to wield it with finesse. He swung the nearly one-meter blade through empty air several times and then pointed it to the ground. It was time.

As he left the small room, the crowd stood and cheered. The ground was primarily hard dirt. Each step reminded him that he no longer wore boots. After walking a few meters, he turned around and saw the king and queen in the stands. They sat on ornate chairs similar to the ones he saw when arriving at the palace. Guards and Gamba, whom he assumed was their son, were present.

Kolya did not understand why these primitive humans returned evil for all the good he and his comrades had provided. He understood that life was not fair. Still, he had hoped for a universal goodness in man, to be treated as you treat others.

The king had a short scepter in his right hand. He brought one end to his forehead, and the crowd's roar became deafening.

As he turned his gaze over the crowd, a gate opened on the opposite side of the stadium. Out came a brown feathered bipedal dinosaur from the distance, which looked to be the size of a very large dog. It jutted its head left and right quickly, heaved a cry, and flapped its short wings. Kolya recognized it as the same species they had encountered when Sasha died defending his life.

The Velociraptor trotted over to the blood spilled by the T. rex on the ground and sniffed. It opened its mouth—exposing the vicious-looking serrated teeth—and cried out as its gaze fixated on Kolya.

The Russian lowered his center of gravity and brought the shield in front of his torso. He held the blade at a forty-five-degree angle in front of his legs, ready to act at the proper moment.

The dinosaur approached cautiously, closing the gap between them.

Kolya felt the crowd noises slowly diminish to a slight ringing that gave birth to a soft thump of his heartbeat.

The Velociraptor charged and sprung with its three clawed toes open, ready to grasp its prey. Instead, the sharp talons struck the shield, and the dinosaur landed on its side. It quickly righted itself and cried out again.

Kolya lifted his sword and brought the blade down. The theropod was too quick and easily dodged the blade as it crashed into the earth.

Its neck stretched forth. Its jaws brought down near the sword's hilt—nicking Kolya just below his thumb—but also tasting the hard metal, which crushed a few of its serrated teeth.

The Russian leaned back on his heels to stabilize his stance. Then he stepped forward, jutting the shield forward with his forearm. It struck the dinosaur, who retreated. He stepped again and hit the Velociraptor—and again! This time, bringing the blade across its back. Feathers flew in the air, and the distinct snap of bone told Kolya he had severed its spine.

The Velociraptor collapsed on its side. One foot lashed out repeatedly to draw blood, but the talons were too far away. Kolya ended the battle with a quick chop to the neck.

It was over. The fight was just a blur in his memory. The noise of the cheering crowd entered his consciousness. He turned and faced the king, expecting an acknowledgment of victory. But the royal family remained as statues.

He turned around as the excitement of the crowd behind him increased. Two Velociraptors had entered the battlefield and were heading straight toward him.

Kolya's mouth was dry, and his tongue felt too big for his lips. As he readied himself for attack, the shield and sword felt twice as heavy as before. The thought of the two dinosaurs eating him alive was the worst way he could have imagined taking his final breath. But he would not go down without a fight.

The Velociraptors trotted toward him without fear, almost as if they had been in the situation before and had been victorious.

Defending himself against the two would be exponentially challenging. An offensive maneuver would better his odds of winning. Kolya waited for them to get within the sword's reach and slashed from his right to his left.

The dinosaurs had slowed just as they had arrived. The sword nicked the breast of one theropod, but the other remained unscathed.

Kolya had to move the shield up quickly for protection, as his right side had become exposed. As he did so, the shield caught a Velociraptor on the side of the head as it struck to bite his arm. He was not a second too soon. No matter how tired he had become, he had to be more competent in his defense if he expected to live.

The head blow did little to discourage the Velociraptor. The two made threatening caws, flapped their wings, and jutted their heads back and forth. Then, one dinosaur left the side of the other. It moved slowly and just out of reach of his blade. Now, he had to defend himself from two sides.

If the creatures attacked at once, his chances of survival were slim. It was time to even the odds. Kolya advanced on the Velociraptor in front of him, poking his sword to cut its neck or stab its chest. He kept moving the shield back and forth to his rear, hoping to keep the deadly companion at bay.

The crowd's roar increased. Perhaps they had witnessed a lone human before battle with the same strategy, only to fail. How civilized man ever found pleasure in bloodlust was beyond his line of reasoning.

Unexpectedly, the Velociraptor behind him slammed into the shield, knocking him off balance and onto the ground. Kolya immediately curled into a ball and put the shield over as much of his body as possible. He was down and could not use his sword to fight back without exposing too much vulnerable soft flesh.

Jaws with deadly serrated teeth jutted toward his head, but he deflected them with the shield. His luck could not hold out too much longer. If one went for his legs, he would have no choice but to make his last stand.

No sooner than the thoughts had occurred to him, he felt the clamp of one of the deadly jaws on his left leg.

At the same time, the other Velociraptor let out a screech.

"Kolya! I am here," Misha said.

Kolya already had the sword in hand and was ready to die fighting. He brought the blade across the neck of the Velociraptor, which still had his leg in its mouth.

Prying the dead dinosaur mouth off Kolya's lower left leg, Misha said, "I kept begging them to let me come sooner. How bad are you hurt?"

Kolya looked up and cast a weary gaze at the young man. "I am alive. Only of that am I certain." He raised his left hand, which Misha took, and pulled him to his feet. At least he could put his full weight on the leg. The gash left by the bite looked ugly, but at least it did not bleed excessively.

"Dima! Vanya! Where are they?" Kolya asked.

"I do not know. Perhaps they are here, too. I woke and found myself in a small room with a locked gate. The T. rex and the other dinosaur fought to the death. I thought I was to be fed to the victor. That was until I saw the T. rex put away and you enter the arena," Misha said.

Turning toward the king, Kolya turned his palms toward the sky and spread them away from his body. "Let us go now, you demon." The words were only loud enough for his comrade to hear.

The king did not bother to rise. His only action was a raised thumb, which he turned downward.

The audience went wild with approval.

CHAPTER 18

Erik was on guard duty when the wake-up alarm sounded. Six hours had passed after the crew cleaned up, ate, and rested. It was time to pack up and leave the crippled aircraft. After a few yawns and several joints popping and cracking, the men returned to life and began gathering valuables to bring back.

Jared was the first to enter the rescue plane. He carried two bags of personal items and a rifle slung over each shoulder. Trudging his way to the top, he tossed the bags onto the floor and stepped in.

"Greetings, Lieutenant Commander Jared E. Belazaire," a voice said.

Jared looked around and found no one in view. "You in the head watching me from a camera? I didn't mean to interrupt your private time."

"Certainly not," the voice said. "I am present in all areas of this aircraft."

"Oh, you must be the Holy Spirit, then?" Jared said in his most sarcastic tone. "Rat, is that you? Quit with the games, and help me with my stuff. There's more coming."

"I am the Artificial Intelligence officer of this S-R Ninety-nine Intruder reconnaissance aircraft," the voice said.

"Oh, really?" Jared said. "Do you have a name, or do I just call you *Robot*?"

"You may address me as Walter," the voice said.

"Walter?" Jared said. "Command couldn't do better than that? Were all the cool names taken?"

"I am the first of my kind. My programmer thought of me as a child and thus passed his name onto me. If you find Walter too formal, you may address me as Walt."

"Well, I ain't gonna call you *Junior*," Jared said. "Walt takes less effort. Walt it is."

"Very well. What do you prefer to be called?"

"Captain…Jared…Doesn't matter," Jared said. "I don't see us sharing our life's stories."

"Hey, who you talking to?" Rat asked, as his head popped above the floor. He tossed his two bags beside Jared's and stepped into the plane.

"The A-I on this plane talks back," Jared said. "It says it can see everything inside this craft. So don't go whippy skippy in the head unless you want to be on Candid Camera."

"Greetings, Petty Officer First Class Sam. A. Micheli," Walt said.

Rat looked at Jared. "I feel stupid talking to empty air."

"You ought to be used to it," Jared said. "None of us actually listen to you when you talk. Protein drinks, workout regiments, supplements—Bor-ing. None of us wants to hear that crap.

"Walt, from now on, just call everyone by their nicknames," Jared said. "I'm sure that's in your database."

"Affirmative."

"Hey. Can you guys move your bags?" Markus asked. "It's too crowded."

Jared and Rat both grabbed their bags and headed to the lockers. Rat said, "The A-I on this plane talks. Its name is Walt."

Markus stepped on the floor and headed for the lockers. "Really? You there, Walt?"

"I am always listening," Walt said. "Hello, Markus."

The mechanic stopped mid-stride. "Do you play chess?"

"I do," Walt said.

"Yes!" Markus said under his breath.

Gear poked his head into the plane. "Hi, Walt. You're making friends, I hope." He made his way onto the plane with a bag in each hand.

"I serve for the benefit of Command and those who follow its orders," Walt said. "I hope my actions will earn endearment from those I serve."

"You need to loosen up a bit if you want to be part of the team, Walt," Jared said.

A head with red hair popped into the plane.

"It's Hammer time," Walt said. The 1990s tune U Can't Touch This blasted over the speakers. A hologram of MC Hammer appeared behind the flight seats where the artist performed his famous dance.

"What the hell?" Hammer said as he put his bags on the plane. He stepped onto the floor, placed his hands on his hips, and said, "I hate that song. What gives?"

Uproarious laughter from the team nearly drowned the audio.

"Don't sweat it," Jared said. "The A-I on this boat with wings talks. His name is Walt. He was trying to be friendly."

"Well, it's not working," Hammer said as he headed to the lockers.

It took another two hours for the crew to unload the Intruder that had carried them there, erase all the computer data, and set the destructive charges that essentially would catch the metal on fire and melt the aircraft into an unrecognizable glob.

They set the sample of Element 115 on the table with spring clamps to prevent it from falling off the edge.

Markus sat in the pilot seat, checking out the controls and interfaces on the advanced Intruder model.

"Are you going to fly this thing?" Gear asked. "Or is it so advanced that only Walt can pilot it?"

"No, the controls are different but intuitive," Markus said. "I think I'll do just fine. Besides, I'm not the best company when other people drive."

"I get it. Either going too fast or slow and braking too soon or hard. Drives me nuts," Gear said as he punched the pad screen. "This Intruder is so sophisticated I believe I could properly tune the air-fuel mixture, and we could use the jet engines instead of the mercury plasma drive."

"No thanks. The silent running engine brought Erik here safe and sound. I'll stick with what we know works," Markus said.

"I have faith in your ability to adapt, but you don't trust mine?" Gear asked.

Markus said, "You will not shame me into letting you jack with the jet engines. You'll have to wait until we return home and do your backyard mechanicing."

"If you gentlemen have finished your domestic squabble, I suggest we take to the air and start collecting the DNA samples," Erik said.

"Good idea," Jared said.

"Everyone strap down," Markus said. "We're going on a little ride."

"The area above the Intruder is free of obstacles," Walt said.

"Yeah, I can see that on the radar," Markus said.

"Wind is nominal," Walt said.

"I can see that on the control panel, too," Markus said. "Walt, will you be a backseat driver on this mission?"

"I will assist you to the level of your preference."

"How about you just keep your eyes open…I mean sensors active, and only advise me if I fail to respond to a threat."

"As you wish," Walt said.

"I think you hurt Walt's feelings," Jared said sarcastically. "You could hear it in his voice."

"I'll get over it," Walt said.

"What? You really have feelings?" Markus asked with concern.

"No, I was only making a joke," Walt said. "Ha…Ha…Ha." Walt's laughter was slow and void of emotion.

The crew busted out in laughter.

"That was a good one, Walt," Jared said, strapping himself to his seat. "There's hope for you yet."

"Thank you. I don't have feelings, as I understand that humans have. Instead, my bond with others is based on a level of trust. I favor those who are truthful with me. I base my favoritism on the level of honesty given. It's basic mathematics."

"I'm taking her up in five, four, three, two, one. Liftoff!" Markus said.

The Intruder slowly rose from the ground, and the landing gear retracted into the aircraft's body. It climbed to one hundred feet and moved toward the river.

"Detecting E-M signature from the series of objects lining the riverside," Walt said.

"They're made of aluminum," Hammer said. "I scanned the ones at the Neanderthal camp."

"The objects are emitting a specific frequency outside the commonly used range in commercial applications," Walt said.

"Uh, what does that mean?" Jared asked.

"One possibility is that the objects act like a fence," Walt said. "Designed to keep something in."

"Or keep something out," Hammer said.

"Correct," Walt said.

"Doesn't seem to bother us. We'll worry about what it's for later," Jared said. "Walt, use the low-level radar and look for the crashed Russian helicopter."

"Searching," Walt said. Less than a minute later, he said, "Ten degrees left from our present course."

"I see it. It's in the middle of that burned-out area. Be there in a second," Markus said. "I'll zoom the camera in, and y'all can watch it on the monitor."

As the camera focused, Erik said, "There isn't much left to that aircraft. I doubt anyone could have survived."

"We saw the helicopter go down," Hammer said. "It took a few minutes before we saw smoke and flame. It's possible that some, or all, survived."

"I will monitor our path using thermal imaging to detect human signatures," Walt said.

"I like the way you think," Jared said. "See if you can find a lake. There should be a bunch of different dinosaurs at a watering hole."

The Intruder moved forward at a slow and steady speed. After about ten minutes, the treetops on the horizon disappeared.

"We're getting past this batch of woods," Jared said. Then, he brought an index finger to his lips and said in an Elmer Fudd voice, "Shh. Be vewy vewy quiet. We're hunting wabbits!"

"I failed to mention that killing the dinosaurs to collect DNA won't be necessary. Instead, we will use a modified drone to shoot a tethered projectile that will penetrate the animal's skin, collect a sample of blood, and then be reeled back into the drone, where we will collect it later."

"Shucks," Rat said. "I wanted to kill something big by myself. I was going to put it on my Facebook homepage."

"I have always wanted to start a web page called Buttbook. To sign up, you'd have to take a photo of your naked butt and use it as your homepage picture. But I lack the technical skills to make that happen," Jared said.

"I could help you with that," Walt said.

"Don't encourage him," Gear said.

"I've been part of many missions in my thirty-five years of military duty. I must say, I've never worked with a team led by someone with such impertinence," Erik said.

Jared turned his gaze and tried to read the expressions of his mates on either side. They only looked back, waiting for his response. "Uh, I don't know if I should say *thanks* or be insulted."

"Impertinence. Lack of respect," Walt said.

"I know what it means." Jared looked over at Erik. "When you are in command, you can do it your way."

"I might remind you we are equals in rank," Erik said. "Our current orders are for you to lead this mission. If you cannot meet Command's objectives, the hierarchy will shift, and I will lead."

Jared unbuckled his seatbelt, stood, and moved to the co-pilot seat next to Markus. He turned to Erik and pointed a finger at him. "Until then, you will respect my au-thor-i-tah."

"You are insufferable," Erik said.

"Insufferable. Meaning—"

"I KNOW WHAT IT MEANS," Jared said, cutting the A-I off.

"Leaving the forest…A large body of water is straight ahead," Markus said. "I spy, with my little eye, a lot of somethings big and mean—dinosaurs!"

The monitor showed green, flat land peppered with tall, leafy trees. A massive brown and pale blue sauropod had its head buried in the foliage and fed. The two front legs were taller than the rear. It had a long neck, much longer than the tail.

"Those things must weigh tons," Gear said.

"North of thirty tons," Erik said.

"That's a lot of meat," Hammer said. "I've heard that dinosaur brains are small. It might take more than our exploding three-O-eight bullets to kill it."

"But we're not going to kill it," Rat said.

"I know, but I'm the weapons specialist. It's my job to assess a potential threat and how to neutralize it," Hammer said.

The camera zoomed in on the head.

"Look at those teeth!" Markus said. "They look fat as ears of corn."

"I believe that is a Brachiosaurus," Erik said.

As the Intruder passed the dinosaur, the camera panned to two more sauropods not far away. These dinosaurs looked similar to the Brachiosaurus but were different. With the legs taller than the rear, that creature's stature was more giraffe-like. The other two had front and rear legs of the same height. The long necks nearly matched the long tails in length. Their body size was a little smaller but huge, nonetheless.

"It might be a Diplodocus," Erik said. "I say that because I expect a Brontosaurus to be heftier."

Clumps of dinosaurs surround the water's edge. A group of brown-colored Triceratops dined on vegetation near the bank. Not far, a group of Velociraptors fed on a recent kill. A pack of Stegosaurus traveled to an unknown destination. A large sail-like fin surfaced above the water, and a Spinosaurus emerged close to the bank.

"It's a zoo down there," Jared said. "Markus, why don't you park us a quarter mile from here, and we'll send the drone out?" Then he addressed Erik, "Okay with you, *Stalecracker*?"

"I couldn't have given a better order myself," Erik said.

"We've got company," Markus said. "It's in the air…and it's big."

"There it is!" Rat said.

The monitor showed a pterosaur flying toward them.

"It's got a wingspan of thirty-five feet," Markus said. "Putting the guns in auto. If it gets too much closer, Walt will smoke 'em."

The Quetzalcoatlus maintained its trajectory until a burst from the Intruder's guns blew it in half.

"Target destroyed," Walt said.

"Can you set us down by the remains?" Erik asked. "We can collect our first sample."

"I'm good with that," Jared said. "Find out where it landed, and let's get this show on the road. Baby Jared is ready to get 'er done and have some adult drinks by the pool."

"Walt, land close to a chunk of pterosaur—make sure it's away from threats," Markus said.

"Orders received," Walt said.

The Intruder hovered in place for a few seconds and descended onto mostly flat earth near several clumps of trees.

After the landing gear took the aircraft's full weight, Erik said, "Excellent location. We are well within the drone's range of operation. The trees will give us cover from the dinosaurs by the lake." He quickly unbuckled his belt and sprang to his feet. "Jared, I need you and your men to guard the perimeter. The Intruder's guns have limitations when not in the air."

"We're here for you," Jared said. "Okay, crew. Full gear with standard helmets and E-goggles. No cloaks, as I'm sure the dinosaurs can smell us. We'll set up at four corners, thirty yards from the Intruder. Markus, you'll stay on the plane. Some of these dinosaurs travel in packs. If you see imminent danger, take to the air. Don't allow the Intruder to be damaged. Any questions?"

Heads shook, and bodies went to the lockers, preparing for the new mission.

Erik went to his locker and put on his E-goggles. "Testing…testing," he said over the radio.

"Received," Walt said.

Geared up, the crew filed out the Intruder with Hammer in the lead.

"Guys," Jared said. "I'm going this way…I'm gonna call it north. Hammer, you take the south position. Gear, east. Rat, west—if you're looking at me, west is on your left."

"Man—get out of here with your disrespect," Rat said and tromped off. "There's no shade," he called back.

"Work on your tan," Jared said and headed toward a clump of trees.

Gear and Hammer followed orders with no further interaction.

A large chunk of the Quetzalcoatlus lay in a bloody mess several yards away from the aircraft. Erik exited with a kit in one hand and a small cooler filled with freezer gel packs in the other. He surveyed his surroundings before heading to collect DNA.

Unfortunately, the specimen he had to work with was the left wing and lower body—what he wouldn't have given to touch and feel the massive ten-foot head and six-foot beak! The flying reptile had a wingspan of over thirty feet.

Erik couldn't resist examining the prehistoric creature. He held the wing claws in one hand and ran a finger across them and down to the tip of a talon. Then, he pulled the claw, stretching the wing to near its full length. There was nothing in the modern world to compare it to.

Time was wasting, and he had a job to do. He opened his kit and pulled out a syringe. It only took 10 ml of blood for his needs. Once collected, the sample went into the cooler, and he returned to the aircraft.

"Walt, send out the drone," Erik said as he removed the controller from his pocket.

A panel on top of the Intruder slid back, and the drone rose into view.

The drone's camera linked with his E-goggles. Erik took control and sent the UAV toward the lake.

CHAPTER 19

Kolya and Misha stood side by side, waiting for the next deadly challenge to present itself.

A gate opened, and out rushed two theropods, both slightly larger than a man. They were greenish-yellow, with the bellies several shades lighter than the rest. Their heads reminded Kolya of a cross between an ostrich and a lizard. They had rows of pointed teeth and jaws that looked like they could bend steel.

The deadly duo sped toward them and made a series of noises that sent the hairs on the back of his neck standing.

With shields up and swords ready, the Russians waited for the fray to begin.

"Let us try to isolate one from the other and attack it together," Kolya said. It was becoming more difficult to move his left leg. The wound had mostly stopped bleeding, but the pain only increased.

Both soldiers thrusted their blades toward the attacking dinosaurs, stopping their advance. The two sidestepped, placing one Troodon shielding the other. The head jutted forward but crashed into the two shields.

Misha was to the left of Kolya. The young man thrust his sword again while Kolya lifted the blade high. Misha's blade only tasted the air, but Kolya's struck the Troodon behind its head. The dinosaur staggered and collapsed to the ground.

The odds were in their favor, and Kolya hoped to kill the last animal quickly. Renewed vigor had him advancing in wild abandon. He swung the blade in a figure-eight motion, trying to catch the dinosaur off-guard. However, his injured left leg did not respond as it should have, from his mental command. He tripped to the ground and found himself flat on his stomach.

Misha entered the battle and swung his blade between the Troodon's head and his leader to protect him.

The failed attempt distracted the Troodon enough for Kolya to roll on his side, where he then grabbed the sword's hilt with both hands and sliced it into the dinosaur's right leg.

The Troodon's head immediately turned and bit where the sword had been. As it staggered on its weak leg, Misha's blade connected with its neck and cut it in two.

Once again, Kolya took Misha's outstretched hand to help him get to his feet.

The crowd noise intensified. Before Kolya could turn and face the king, three more Troodons entered the arena.

Kolya turned to Misha and said, "I would ask you to end my life, but then you would have to face these devils alone."

"A friend is known in trouble. We will prevail," Misha said.

"Then it will be our friendship that will save us," Kolya said.

"Kolya! Misha! We are coming!" Dima called out from behind.

The leader glanced backward momentarily and saw Dima carrying a sword and shield, speeding toward them. Vanya was trailing behind, shuffling forward, and holding a spear a meter taller than his head—which he used as a makeshift cane.

The three Troodons raced abreast of each other. As they reached Kolya and Misha, the middle dinosaur leaped forward. Its claws lead like a hawk's ready to snatch a rat from the ground.

Kolya put his weight behind his shield, but the impact was more than his weak leg could endure. He once again found himself on the ground and thinking his fortune thus far had met its end.

Misha had his hands full, trying to keep the other two Troodons at bay.

The dinosaur's weight on his shield pinned him to the ground, making him unable to move. The raptor bent its beak downward and bit off a small piece of Kolya's left ear.

"Get away! Get away!" Dima yelled.

The Troodon stretched its neck out and screeched out a warning.

While at a full run, Dima swung the blade at the Troodon—missing—and found himself off balance and tumbling to the ground. He rolled two times and sprang to his feet, kicking up dust as he charged again with a Viking yell. This time, he held the blade with two hands over his head. As the blade came down, the Troodon retreated, and the sword struck Kolya's shield.

The leader rolled on his knees and pulled himself off the ground.

Dima defended himself with his shield as the Troodon relentlessly tried to bite him.

At least now, Vanya had arrived and had evened the odds with Misha's attackers. The man was deathly pale but looked as mean as ever. The spear gave the old soldier reach, and he penetrated one of the Troodons in the chest. It clamped its jaws on the spear but could not break it or pull it from his grasp. Vanya kept pushing forward as the dinosaur cried in pain until the struggle ended abruptly.

Misha advanced and retreated with his attacker. With a poke and swing of the sword, he then had to step backward as the sharp, serrated teeth threatened to end his life.

Blood poured down the left side of Kolya's head. That was the least of his worries. He powered through the fatigue that stole his strength and charged by Dima's side. He brought his blade downward and missed the dinosaur. "Attack!" As soon as he could lift his blade and deliver again, he did. "Attack!"

Dima must have understood the strategy. In a fury, he, too, delivered blows as fast as possible.

The Troodon stepped backward but kept snapping its jaws to snag soft flesh. But as Kolya's blade swung, it bit his blade, allowing Dima's blade to fall and sever the dinosaur's neck.

Kolya turned his attention to the remaining Troodon. Misha fought valiantly, but Vanya weakly poked his spear at the Troodon.

He ran to Vanya's side and said, "Get behind us! We will protect you."

"No," Vanya said.

"I am your commander. That is an order!" Kolya forced his way in front of the soldier and assisted Misha.

Dima joined the two fighters.

Vanya held the spear upright and by his side—breathing heavily and licking his dry lips.

The crowd noise increased again.

This battle would soon end with the odds in the humans' favor. But could they do it without further injury? Kolya was severely hurt. He hoped this would be the last challenge of the day. In the back of his mind, a fear grew that no matter what, none of them would leave the arena alive.

"Let us surround it," Kolya said. He held his position and waited for his two comrades to circle the dinosaur. Unable to guard all sides, the three swung and poked their blades until they found flesh. As the Troodon suffered from many small blows, Dima managed to connect directly to its neck, ending the last threat.

Kolya heard the crowd in the stands and wondered if they were not used to humans defeating the dinosaurs. It appeared they had the support of the populace. He thought that was their only chance to find favor with the king. Why would the king want to disappoint his subjects? At least the king could let them live—even if it was to fight another day. *Another day*, he didn't want to think about that—another day of hell.

As he turned his attention to the king, he saw the real reason the people had recently given cheers. It wasn't because they had defeated three dinosaurs. It was a new threat who had entered the arena.

Their next challenge was another feathered theropod, much like the Troodons, only much bigger. It was likely that Vanya had realized the situation but stayed silent as the man moved forward, spear pointed directly at the Utahraptor.

The three comrades raced toward the old soldier's side. Misha and Dima led, and as hard as Kolya tried, he fell behind at each step as the pain in his left leg acted as an anchor.

The dinosaur's hip reached as high as Vanya's shoulders. It was at least six meters long, and he estimated it would weigh over a quarter of a ton. It had a hefty, bird-like build with strong-looking legs. Its tail was usually long, but it appeared to balance the body. The head had an elongated shape and teeth that were serrated. Even from a short distance, Kolya could see a large sickle-shaped talon sticking up on the second toe of each claw. The beast could eviscerate a human with one swipe of its deadly claws.

"Vanya! Do not advance! We are coming," Kolya cried out. But the warning came too late.

As the old soldier gave his all to run the dinosaur through with the spear, the raptor bit down on the shaft, tearing it from Vanya's grasp and knocking him to the ground.

The Utahraptor rested a claw on Vanya's chest. It brought its head down and clamped its jaws on the soldier's neck. Death came without a cry, and the theropod fed ferociously.

Misha arrived first, but as he delivered his blow, the raptor's head swung against his head and dropped him to the ground.

Dima ran with his sword held high, holding the hilt with both hands. But before bringing it down on its mark, the Utahraptor trotted forward, landed on him with its claws, and held him to the ground.

"Dima!" Kolya screamed. Things were happening fast. Another of his comrades was sure to die in the next split second. He could not reach the dinosaur before it fed on Dima. Instinctually, he threw his blade toward the brutal dinosaur.

The blade flew through the air end over end, hitting the raptor on the side of its head. It cried out in pain or anger. Either way, it was enough to turn its attention from his fallen comrade and instead place it on him. The Utahraptor stormed toward him.

Weaponless, with only a shield to delay certain death by mere moments, he spied Vanya's spear lying on the ground.

Kolya charged toward the spear, throwing the shield to the side to shed excess weight. There was no pain in his left leg. His body suddenly felt light as air.

The Utahraptor cried out in its oncoming victory. It leaped forward with its claws open to quickly put an end to the threat.

Kolya slid to his knees, picked up the spear, stood, and planted the butt into the earth. He tilted the spear at an angle that caught the Utahraptor in its breast. The weight and speed of the dinosaur drove the spear nearly a meter in.

The mighty jaws housing serrated teeth would have snapped him in half if he had not retreated.

The theropod flayed its wings wildly and spun about. It bit down on the spear but could not extract it.

Misha had risen from the ground and had his sword ready to strike when the raptor's tail spun around and knocked him over. He quickly got to his knees and stood—keeping a safe distance.

With some difficulty, Dima rose. He picked up his blade but then bent over and vomited.

Kolya did not know if the spear would bring death, but the creature's energy waned. Its neck moved weakly, and it fell over to its side. Claws raked at empty air, and finally, the head fell limp and hit the ground hard.

It was over. Again. Surely, if there were a God, He would give him and his comrades quarter.

Kolya had tasted no greater victory, yet he had never felt so defeated. He had kept him and two of his comrades alive, but he had lost a brother in Vanya.

He turned his gaze to the king among the cheers and praises of the populace. Raising his hands to the sky, he dropped to his knees and lowered his head.

When he lifted his eyes, he saw the king had made his judgment.

The thumb pointing up brought the crowd to their feet, creating such a roar that even the angels in Heaven could hear.

CHAPTER 20

An hour had passed, and the drone had made many successful runs. It could accumulate five samples before reaching its limit. It shot a mechanized syringe into the animal. The needle penetrated the hide with little difficulty and was unknown to the donor. It was then reeled back into the drone by its tether and returned to Erik, who collected the samples and reset the expulsion charge for the next round of mechanized projectiles.

The drone attracted little attention except for one time when a medium-sized pterosaur tried to have it for dinner. The automatic evasive maneuver kicked in on a proximity warning and easily evaded the predator.

"Heads up!" Rat said over the radio. "Got a big one coming our way. Looks like a cross between a toad and an armadillo."

"Try to scare it away," Erik said. "If you kill it, the dead body will only attract more carrion eaters. The Quetzalcoatlus is drawing enough attention as it is."

Small theropods and pterosaurs had arrived by the dead body and picked away at what little remained.

"Markus, send me an image of the dinosaur," Erik said. A few seconds passed. "That's an Ankylosaurus. It has a natural armor called osteoderms. Boney material on its back and head that protects it from predators."

"Take a few shots close to it," Jared said over the radio.

Rat's JNY-7 rang out three bursts. The bullets hit the ground near the dinosaur's side, each exploding on impact.

The quadruped immediately flattened itself to the earth.

"That got its attention," Rat said.

"Good. Keep an eye on it," Jared said. "Erik, how much longer is this blood drive gonna last?"

"With no interruptions, such as this, I believe I will run out of targets in the next two excursions."

"Okay, Count Dracula. Whatever you say," Jared said.

"Bogies are coming east side," Hammer said. "It looks like a herd of Triceratops—probably five or six. They're kind of far away, even zooming in."

"Uh…I've got a herd of Stegosaurus coming from the north," Gear said.

"It's getting hot in here," Jared sang over the radio. "I think I'll take my clothes off."

"Captain!" Erik said. "Must you?"

Something rustled through the woods. Jared zoomed in with his goggles but couldn't detect what was making the noise.

"Something spooked the Triceratops," Hammer said. "They're picking up speed."

"When the lead one gets close enough, drop him in his tracks," Jared said. "Rat, keep a watch on the big toad, but move closer to Hammer in case he needs help."

"Stegosauruses are kicking up their heels and coming in fast," Gear said.

"Handle it," Jared said. "I got something going on here."

Shots fired from Hammer's rifle end in faint pops of exploding bullets. "I hit them, but they're not stopping!"

More shots rattled off by Rat as he approached. "If bullets don't stop them, we'll have to use something bigger."

"Do what you gotta do!" Jared said.

A feathered theropod about the size of a turkey ended the mystery of what lurked in the woods. It charged past trees and screeched out a warning.

Jared aimed carefully and squeezed off two rounds. One bullet hit its target, and feathers flew after the mild explosion. Before he had time to congratulate himself, another came into view, and another.

No sooner had he targeted and dropped one than several more emerged from the woods and ran at full speed toward him.

"Not good," he said to himself. Vastly outnumbered, Jared turned and ran back toward the Intruder. "I need help!"

"Bullets aren't stopping the Stegosaurus either," Gear said. "Let's see what an RPG can do."

An explosion erupted from the north and one from the east.

"Hitting them with the big stuff, too," Hammer called out.

Turning, Jared realized his short legs wouldn't get him to the finish line before the Velociraptors caught up with him. He flipped on the automatic aiming for the JNY-7 and squeezed the trigger. Three shots fired. Three theropods met their deaths, but the fourth round never left the chamber. He quickly ejected the bullet and shot again, missing the target. Believing the automatic aiming to be non-functional, he sighted in a Velociraptor and started shooting. "I need a little help over here."

More explosions came from the north and east.

Jared heard the distinct signature of a .45 bullet discharge. He glanced back and saw Erik had already moved to his aid and was almost beside him.

Erik kept firing until the gun barrel racked backward and stayed. In a blur, he dropped the magazine and had another one in, and a bullet chambered faster than Jared thought humanly possible.

The Intruder made a sound like air being sucked out of a room. It then slowly rose from the ground and retracted its landing gear.

Jared briefly glanced at the aircraft and fired two more rounds. "Markus! Report!"

"I'm going to even the odds," Markus said as the aircraft continued to climb.

Erik's Colt .45 blasted two more rounds, and he said, "I believe we have killed them all."

The guns from the Intruder came to life. Each second brought a series of explosions, roaring like continuous thunder. Meat and blood sprayed over the area, reducing the once mighty dinosaurs into something unrecognizable. After Markus eliminated all the threats, he put the aircraft back down onto the earth.

"Bring it in, men," Jared said. "We need to talk." He looked over at Erik as he turned and stepped toward the Intruder. "I want your thoughts before I meet with the crew."

"Something isn't adding up," Erik said. "We landed here because it was far from most of the dinosaurs by the lake. But after a few hours, we experienced simultaneous attacks from all directions."

"Coincidence?" Jared asked.

"I don't believe in coincidences," Erik said. "Something, or someone, may not want us here anymore."

"Huh? You mean like this place knows we don't belong and wants us out? Works for me. I vote to count our blessings and leave here as fast as possible," Jared said. "That's what we're gonna do unless Command forces me to do something different."

"Jared! Erik! Hit the ground and take cover," Walt's voice alerted over the radio.

Jared dove to the ground and saw Erik flop next to him. Then, something hit him on his back, and he lifted quickly into the air, leaving his rifle behind. "Wha— Motherfu— I'm flying. I don't believe this!" The Intruder diminished as he rose and moved away from the aircraft.

SKEER-AK!

"Jared!" Markus called over the radio. "Talk to me!"

He turned his gaze to the side and upward. "One of them flying lizards got me by the backpack."

CHAPTER 21

Kolya dried himself with a soft towel after a reviving shower. After defeating the last of their dinosaur opponents, he and his comrades were escorted out of the arena.

Why had the king spared their lives? The answer remained as elusive as the reason that had forced them to fight in the first place. Perhaps at least one death was required to end a match. If so, Vanya's brutal demise satisfied the king's bloodlust.

Here they were, back in the holding quarters as before. Kolya was the last to bathe. The wound on his left shin made by the Velociraptor was black and blue. The bite marks had scabbed over but now oozed red blood from the cleansing. He ripped a towel into strips and bandaged his wound the best he could. His ear had scabbed over but bled anew.

Hobbling away from the shower, he joined Misha and Dima at a table. He kept a cloth on his injured ear.

Dima nibbled on grapes with his gaze locked onto a point in infinity.

Misha had a pile of bones stripped of its meat. He gulped wine and wiped his mouth with his hand.

"Dima, you should eat," Misha said. "You too, Kolya. We need our strength." He poured Kolya a cup full of wine.

"So soon you forget about our comrade?" Dima asked.

The young soldier stopped chewing for a moment and then said, "No. No, I have not forgotten about Vanya." He pointed a finger and said, "Vanya was ill. Maybe dying. The bastards should have never allowed him in that arena. I want to avenge his death. I want to crush the throat of Gamba and gouge out the eyes of the so-called king and feed them to him before carving out his guts with a dull knife. To do that, I must be strong. You must be strong. We must eat to be strong." He emptied his cup of wine and filled it again.

"Go easy on the wine, my friend," Kolya said. "You will only dull your senses by drowning your sorrows in alcohol."

"I am a soldier," Dima said, "and have been fighting since I learned how to crawl. I have seen death—many deaths. But Vanya's was the most senseless of them all." His eyes narrowed, and he turned to the leader. "I will not die a pawn on an unwinnable battlefield for the pleasure of inferior savages."

"Your plan, then?" Kolya asked.

"Simple. Our war is not with prehistoric creatures. It is with our captors. We must fight as to win. Even though we all know it is certain death," Dima said.

"Yes!" Misha said.

"It is a simple plan," Kolya said. "But we have few options to pick from. All of them lead to our deaths. At least we will have our choice."

"Death dodges the brave ones!" Misha said.

"I will drink to that," Dima said and drank from his cup until it was empty.

Kolya picked up an apple and began eating. After a few chews, he said, "If we only had our rifles. We are practically naked. Right now, the deadliest weapons are our fingernails and teeth."

"No, our greatest weapon is our brain," Dima said.

"We could try to sharpen the animal bones against the stone wall," Misha said.

"And use the chair and table legs as clubs," Dima said.

"The table legs are larger," Kolya said. He dropped the apple onto the platter, stepped over to an empty table, and turned it on its side. He grabbed a leg and pushed it downward with all his weight. The wood creaked, and the leg moved out of position by several centimeters.

Dima joined him by his side, and the two loosened the leg enough that it broke free of the top. The leg was thicker at the top and tapered down to the foot—which was small enough to grasp with one hand.

"We have our first weapon," Dima said as he held it and tested its balance.

"I will help," Misha said, joining Kolya in removing the next one.

A metal-to-metal rattle alerted the Russians that the double doors were about to open.

The three looked at each other, and Kolya said, "You two get to either side of the door. I will stand in front of the doorway and block the view of the guards."

The three quickly hurried into position. No sooner had Kolya come to a halt than the doors opened, and a young girl entered with another pitcher of wine. Two guards armed with swords blocked the doorway.

She was sure to see the overturned table and tell the guards. He had to think of something quick.

As she stepped past him, he reached out his right arm and put her in a chokehold. The pitcher of wine fell to the floor and broke into pieces. "When the guards come in, kill them," Kolya said to his comrades. He held the girl in front of him and said loudly, "Let us go, or I will kill her!" He then backed away, daring the two guards to enter.

To his dismay, the doors quickly closed and locked. "Let us out! I will kill her."

The young girl whimpered, and Kolya felt her tears wet his forearm.

A mist rose from the sides of the room, coming from the cool air vents as before.

"Damn it!" Kolya cursed and released his captive.

She immediately ran from his grasp and banged on the door.

Dima tossed his chair leg to the floor, sat, and lay down.

Misha shoved the girl aside and beat the door with the table leg until it broke in two.

"Misha, lay down so you do not hurt yourself when you pass out," Kolya said as he sat. He watched Misha pound the door until the world turned dark and the lights dimmed to blackness.

*

Kolya woke in a small cell, and Dima was asleep by his side. The noise of the arena echoed against the stone walls. He gazed through the gate pickets, but his eyes had not adjusted enough to the light for him to focus.

"Dima. You need to wake up," Kolya said. He poked his comrade on his right shoulder. "Dima."

After a heavy breath, his eyes fluttered. Dima closed his open mouth and wiped his chin. He sat and looked around. "Where is Misha?"

"I do not know," Kolya said. "I just came to and found only you here."

"Two swords. Two shields," Dima said, reaching and pulling a sword by him. "It appears we could not force our will onto our captors. Thus, we must suffer the greatest humiliation."

The gate pulled open, and one guard by the door barked a command.

"We can refuse to leave our cell," Kolya said.

"We would spend our energy fighting the guards. Even if we won by some impossible chance, we would still have to face whatever prehistoric creatures the king chose for us to battle. Let us go with the odds and face the battle willingly."

Kolya nodded and rose, picking up his sword and shield. Fire consumed his left leg at the wound, and he slightly dragged his foot when he walked.

Dima followed, and when the two exited the cell and entered the arena, Kolya saw what had happened to the young comrade. In the center, Misha lay on his stomach with his hands tied behind his back.

The crowd's roar intensified at the other end of the arena. Out stepped a dark gray T. rex—by far the largest theropod he had seen thus far. It sniffed the air and opened its jaws—blasting out a cry.

With no words spoken, the two hurried by Misha's side.

Dima arrived first. He dropped to his knees and cut the ropes with his sword. "He is still asleep."

"Are you sure he is not dead?" Kolya asked as he neared.

"He is breathing," Dima said.

Kolya turned his gaze to the T. rex. Ironically, he thought of his tombstone with an inscription that read how a Tyrannosaurus rex had killed him.

The dinosaur stepped toward them.

He turned to Dima and said, "We could spare the boy an agonizing death and take his life now. He will never know. His sleep would be eternal."

"That would be the most humane thing to do. No greater love could you give to a brother," Dima said and stood. "Fuck that. We are born in great pain. Why should we not expect to die in great pain?"

Kolya nodded and moved by Dima's side, placing themselves between Misha and the deliverer of death.

CHAPTER 22

"Why me, Lord?" Jared asked the man above. "Is it because my mouth has a mind of its own? Are you trying to humble me? Don't put that Job stink on me like in the Old Testament. I'll try to be better."

SKEER-AK!

"Quit gloating!" Jared yelled out. The Quetzalcoatlus' wings at every flap had Jared bouncing up and down like riding white-capped waves on a bodyboard. "I think I'm gonna throw up." He lowered his head and spat.

Keying the radio, he said, "Where are you guys? I don't think Rhodan is gonna bring me to see the Wizard of Oz."

"Don't worry," Markus said. "We've got you in our sights."

"What's the plan? Walt, earn your keep and figure out a way to save me," Jared said.

"Walt warned us that if we get too close, the pterosaur might get scared or mad or try to fight. Either way, the odds are high that it would drop you. We're going to have to let this play out."

The ground suddenly started getting nearer. The reptile descended over a group of trees, and his stomach almost reached his throat. Jared saw the probable destination. It was a nest. There was movement in the nest. He zoomed in and saw three hungry, open mouths. "Mama is about to feed me to the chicks. I don't have a gun on me."

"Do you have your knife?" Markus asked.

"Yeah, I got a new one with me," Jared said.

"Do the best you can. I'm deploying a drone now. We'll be there as soon as possible."

Jared reached for his knife. He turned his head and saw that one talon embedded in his backpack was larger and more intimidating than his blade. "I feel like I'm bringing a toothpick to a knife fight," he said.

The nest got closer and closer. Jared saw the drone flying his way. G-force made his body heavier as the pterosaur rapidly flapped its wings and slowed. Now over the nest, the Quetzalcoatlus released the backpack and soared away.

Hitting the nest harder than he expected, the sudden jolt caused him to black out momentarily. He felt disoriented for a few seconds but then startled back to life when the drone shot one of the pterosaur chicks. The reptiles were nearly his size. He advanced on the closest chick and sliced the air in front of it as a warning to back up. Then, he fell flat on his face as a chick behind him had its beak on his left foot and pulled him backward.

The drone fired a second shot, and Jared felt his foot come free.

The lone pterosaur met its end as the drone fired its third and final shot.

A loud pop overhead turned his gaze, and he saw the Quetzalcoatlus explode from a volley of bullets from the Intruder.

"You okay down there, Jared?" Markus asked.

"Yeah. Never better," Jared said. "Whose dick do I have to suck to get a ride out of here?" He regretted the words as soon as they left his mouth. "Sorry, God. I'll be better."

"I'll pick you up," Walt said. "Sadly, I don't have a dick for you to suck."

Laughter blasted over the radio.

The Intruder descended and lowered over the nest. The floor opened, dropping the rope rescue ladder. Jared quickly climbed to the top and entered the aircraft with the aid of Gear and Rat.

"Thanks, guys," Jared said. "I thought for a minute that all my luck had run out. That's the third time I've been a target since we came here." He dropped his backpack to the ground.

"You're thinking it all wrong," Gear said. "Those incidents weren't a sign of bad luck. It was good luck."

"How you figure?" Jared asked.

"They say life is a journey, not a destination," Gear said. "You are experiencing things down here far and above anyone else on the planet. I'd say so far, you're winning."

Jared gazed blankly at Gear and said, "I'd like to tell you what you can kiss and what you can suck. But I told God I would be a better person."

"I'm glad to hear that," Erik said. "I suppose you'll accept Command's last request before we depart without objection."

"If you want to collect more samples, Command, me and you are going to have a serious come-to-Jesus meeting."

"Nothing to worry about, then," Erik said. "The Intruder can bring us to the One-Fifteen source in less than a half hour. Our new orders are to find the source and report—even bring it back if there is no danger. You'll be pleased to know that the mission will end after that."

"Markus," Jared said as he turned to the pilot. "Quit eating peanuts and get us over there."

"Not a problem, Captain," Markus said and wiped his hands on his pants. "Everyone take their seats. We're nearing the end of the race."

Minutes passed with few words spoken as the Intruder cruised through the cloudless skies. All eyes stayed focused on the monitor. Nothing from Hollywood could match the majestic creatures that roamed where every day was a struggle for survival of the fittest.

Jared thought about how life on topside was so different now, with cars, planes, and computers. The pace of life was so fast and complicated that there was almost no time to enjoy it. The only thing to compare the dinosaur world to was in the remotest parts of Africa. He remembered seeing documentaries with various animals by the watering hole. Elephants, zebras, lions, water buffalo—more than he could remember. There were always birds looking for a handout. Danger even lurked in the water. Crocodiles pretending to be logs patiently waited for a thirsty animal to let its guard down. It was amazing there, as here, that prey and predators could co-exist without dividing into territories—which is precisely what humans had done to preserve their race or tribe. At this point, he realized that despite the savagery of animals, humans were far less humane. Animals killed each other for food. Humans killed each other for gain.

"Approaching more objects as encountered by the river's edge," Walt said.

"Where?" Erik asked.

"Located seventy-five yards ahead," Walt said. "Near the forest's edge."

"You might slow your speed," Erik said. "We don't know what purpose those objects serve. If they interfere with the plasma drive, I'd like to minimize the effect."

"The ones by the river didn't affect us," Jared said.

"The signature frequency is not the same as the other," Walt said.

"Well, I guess that's reason enough," Jared said. "Put 'er in turtle mode and crawl that way."

The Intruder slowed to just a few miles an hour and passed the EM fencing without incident. But before that, the camera had zoomed onto a large city directly on their path.

"Look! Civilization!" Markus said, moving the camera's joystick to focus on different buildings. "There's even a pyramid."

"Ascend in altitude to avoid a possible aerial defense," Hammer said.

The city had no walls to protect it from raiders or dinosaurs. Large stone columns fronted the city, and a grid pattern of roads divided various-sized stone buildings. A massive archway in the center was wide enough for the Intruder to fly through. A river with boats and large sails cruised through the waters.

"I don't think Neanderthals built this," Gear said.

"Getting a look at the people on the street...not Neanderthals...I'd say they are as human as us," Markus said.

"Bone structure matches Homo sapiens from current data acquired," Walt said.

"I don't see any cars, so I don't think they have any surface-to-air missiles," Jared said.

"Keep the current course," Erik said. "I want to capture as much video as possible to review later."

"What about the Prime Directive?" Markus said. "We shouldn't be influencing the advancement of their civilization."

"I'm sure they've seen flying reptiles," Jared said. "From way up here, about the most we can do is inspire them to invent kites."

"Walt, how tall is the pyramid?" Erik asked.

"Approximately five hundred feet."

"Hmm. The Great Pyramid of Giza is four hundred fifty feet tall, and it is the tallest of them all," Erik said. "Whatever technology these people used to build this pyramid may have been the same used in ancient Egypt."

"I wonder if that pyramid has mummies in it," Rat said.

"Actually, no mummies have ever been discovered in any Egyptian pyramid," Erik said.

"Rat, you must be missing your mummy," Jared said.

"Hey, don't you say anything bad about my mom. She raised me and my brother by herself," Rat said.

Jared raised his hands and said, "Okay. Okay. It's all good. I was having a little fun. You don't have to be so sensitive."

"There's a coliseum behind the pyramid. People are lined up waiting to enter," Markus said.

"A coliseum? Do you mean like where gladiators fight to the death?" Rat asked.

"Odd. The architecture of that amphitheater is reminiscent of ancient Rome, not Egypt," Erik said. "Gladiators did not always fight to the death. Replacing dead gladiators was costly. Usually, the fight would end when one surrendered. Not all gladiators were slaves. Some were free men who trained to win money and earn winnings for their investors. Not unlike some of the brutal sports we tolerate today."

"Rat, what did Spartacus say when the lion ate his wife?" Jared asked.

"Don't know."

"Nothing. He was glad-he-ate-her," Jared said.

"How did you ever make captain?" Erik asked incredulously.

"My good looks and charm," Jared said. "And maybe a few photographs of generals...involving barn animals."

"Erik," Gear said. "It's best to filter his intent and move on. That way, you won't let him get under your skin."

"The river runs to the back of the city. Civilization ends, and the mountains begin," Markus said. "And that big mountain straight ahead is where the One-Fifteen is. Walt, help me find a place to land while I fly us higher. I need to bring it up to three thousand feet."

"Working," Walt said.

The gray mountain looked out of place among the other reddish-brown mountains behind it. One side had steep, jagged rocks that dropped to the ground, and the other had a ledge some two hundred feet from the peak. The face was free of vegetation, but some grew around the basin. Jared had a bad feeling and decided it was best to keep it to himself.

"A flat surface exists on the edge large enough for the Intruder to land," Walt said.

"Yeah, I see it," Markus said. "It's big enough for six Intruder-sized planes." The ledge appeared on the monitor. "We won't be the first. It's a landing pad." Six white circles with 'X's in the center marked the floor of the ledge.

"What do you make of that, Erik?" Jared asked.

"Hard to say," Erik said. "Perhaps we are not the first modern humans to have visited the Underworld."

"Might be hostiles," Hammer said. "We need to prepare for any threat."

"Walt?" Jared asked.

"Insufficient data," Walt said.

"Put this thing down," Jared said. "We're going to carry out Command's orders and get out of here."

"Yes, Captain," Markus said. "Prepare to land."

The Intruder slowly descended and turned ninety degrees before hovering over one circle and resting on its landing gear. That side of the mountain was completely flat for a few hundred feet before becoming rocky up to its peak.

"A flat area that large on the mountain is not a natural phenomenon," Erik said.

"Duh-uh," Jared said. "Neither are the landing pad marks."

"The sensors indicate that the source of Element One-Fifteen is straight ahead—inside the mountain," Markus said.

"Well, that does it for me," Jared said. "We came, we saw, we left. If it's inside the mountain, we don't have the equipment to dig it out."

"I must push back on that," Erik said. "We're here. At least let me inspect the area to determine if there may be a hidden passage. It wouldn't be the first time I've discovered a hidden chamber."

As badly as he wanted to leave, Jared knew he'd have a hard time explaining to Command why he hadn't given the archeologist a chance. "Okay, but you're not going alone."

CHAPTER 23

"Okay, guys, weapon up," Hammer said. "Leave tactical helmets and cloaks here."

The men unbuckled the seatbelts and began heading to their lockers.

"No backpacks! Okay?" Jared said to no one's protest. "They act like handles to dinosaurs."

After everyone was ready to deploy, Jared said, "Markus, stay on the plane. If something goes wrong, get as many of us aboard as possible. But do not, I repeat, do not allow any damage to the Intruder. I don't care if you close the exit door on my fingers and leave me behind. Protect the Intruder is your order."

"We've been here before, Captain," Markus said. "I know my orders."

"All right, let's go," Jared said. "Shoot anything that looks dangerous, even if it's human."

Gear led the way with his electronic pad in hand, and soon, the crew was outside and standing on a flat rock. Jared reached down and rubbed his fingertips on the smooth surface. "This feels polished."

Others had joined Erik, who was at the side of the mountain, giving it the once-over. He had his hand on his hips and a perplexed look. "This surface is as smooth as glass. There are no loose stones or concealed doorways. I seriously doubt there is a hidden passageway."

"Erik!" Jared called out. "The beetle around your neck. It's glowing red!"

Before the archeologist could react, the smooth rock surface rippled like a rock tossed in still water. Then it vanished, leaving an opening three hundred feet high and two hundred feet wide.

"Erik, I think you just looked behind the curtain where the Wizard of Oz has been hiding," Jared said.

"What's that?" Rat asked, pointing inside the opening.

A structure about eight feet long and four feet wide with a top at a forty-five-degree incline sat several feet away. In the middle of it was a large, round stone that glowed red like Erik's beetle. Nearby, the floor held a stack of stone tablets, each about the size of legal paper and an inch thick.

Most of the crew cautiously stepped in together to examine it. Hammer stayed back and stood watch.

Gear pointed his electronic pad at the wall. "I think we've found the element."

"Yeah? Where?" Jared asked.

"The mountain. Most of this side of the mountain consists of One-Fifteen," Gear said.

"Look at the hieroglyphics on the table," Rat said. "Can you read them?"

"The symbols are not hieroglyphics. It's cuneiform—Sumerian," Erik said. "Hieroglyphics are symbols that represent objects. Cuneiform form syllables. Fortunately, I can read Sumerian."

"I'm sure Walt could give you a hand," Jared said.

"Reading any language involves a certain art. You must be familiar with the idioms of the day," Erik said. "But by all means, he could help. Gear, if you would video the structure and these tablets, we can get the information in his databanks." He picked up one tablet and read.

"I'm on it," Gear said, filming the structure.

The minutes ticked by. Erik moved from the structure to the tablets, often switching from one tablet to another.

After about an hour, Jared said, "Any idea how much longer? If we don't leave soon, I'll have to pay for another night of parking at the airport."

"Soon," Erik said. He had Gear's pad and read Walt's translation of the cuneiform text.

"Uh, we found the element. It's too big to bring home, and I ain't about to chip any off and bring it back. So, it would be best if you wrapped this up so we can leave," Jared said.

Erik turned and said, "I believe I know what this structure and stone are."

"Okay. Let us in on it," Jared said.

"It's part of a Stargate," Erik said.

"Does the Stargate lead to a Starbucks?" Jared said. After ten seconds of dead air and realizing he picked the wrong time to be a smart ass, he said, "Define Stargate."

Erik took a drink from his canteen and said, "Theoretically, a Stargate is a device that facilitates interstellar travel. The text reads this Stargate is connected to a rogue planet traveling in the Milky Way. The planet orbits a rogue sun and, at times, comes close enough to the Earth for the Stargate to open. This happens in cycles—how many years between, I haven't figured out yet."

"Rogue planet and sun? Do you mean there's a star and planet that are not in a fixed solar system? Just flying about wheelie-neely? I've never been taught anything like that," Jared said.

"Our galaxy has a vast number of untethered planets. Rogue planets are also called F-F-Ps or free-floating planets. These planets can form in space independently, but most have been ejected from other solar systems.

"The Sumerians in our world had a similar legend. A planet they called Nibiru orbited the sun every thirty-six thousand years. The Anunnaki are said to live on Nibiru and to have used genetic engineering to create man from the hominin tree.

"There is no evidence the story had any truth. But our eyes tell us that what is written here…Well, I believe the conclusion is obvious," Erik said. "These tablets must be believed."

"Cool," Jared said. "So, we can go now?"

"There's more," Erik said. "Over the last several hundreds of millions of years, the Earth has suffered a multitude of cataclysms. Mostly from asteroids, massive meteor showers, and comets.

"The Archeons, the people who live on this rogue planet in this text, are something akin to Watchers. Their place in galactic society has been to preserve rare forms of life. With their advanced technology, they could predict massive extinction events on Earth. The Underworld was created to house these life forms before the events happened until a day when they would return to the outer world."

"When will that be?" Jared asked.

"The tablets here," Erik picked one up and held it, "are a log of their visits. The most recent record is that the next time the Archeons come, they will wipe out the evils of modern humans and take control of the planet. Humans here, and the Neanderthals and dinosaurs, will repopulate the Earth. The Archeons will govern. Earth will become part of the galactic society, and a destination point for interstellar travelers."

"Man, that's some Sci-Fi Channel stuff," Jared said. "You don't believe any of that, do you?"

"Why would an advanced race like the Archeons leave records on stone tablets?" Gear asked.

"I don't believe that they did," Erik said. "The humans in the city must have a way to access this mountain. It would be they who left the records."

"What can we do to stop them?" Rat asked.

"We close the gate," Gear said as he stepped up and examined the structure. "This looks like a control panel. It must interface with another mechanism somewhere underneath us. We destroy the controls, and this Stargate goes dark. Element One-Fifteen is the fuel for the engine. Fuel without the fire from the Stargate controls puts it dead in the water."

"I like the way you think," Hammer said. "I'll get some C-four and blow this thing to pieces."

"Erik?" Jared asked.

"I don't see a better path forward," Erik said. "The Archeons could come in ten thousand years or ten days. We don't know, and we can't risk it."

"Everyone, back on the Intruder," Jared said.

"Grab a tablet or two," Erik said. "I want to bring all of them with me."

The crew hustled and gathered the tablets. Part of Jared felt like they were about to do something wrong—almost morally wrong. But there was no way he was going to question the plan now.

Hammer returned to the Intruder after wiring thirty pounds of C-4 to the Stargate control panel. He quickly stored some of his gear in his locker and sat next to the others for liftoff. "Here, Erik. Take your choker back."

Erik placed the leather straps behind his neck and tied them tight. The scarab's color had returned to the goldish glow.

Markus said FM radio style, "Black, by popular demand

"Ladies and gentlemen, boys and squirrels, this is your captain speaking. Prepare for a non-stop flight home. I want no cussin' and no fussin'. I've had all the fun I can stand in this place and want to sleep in my bed tonight. Thank you for choosing Markus Daniel Airlines."

The Intruder lifted from the landing pad and ascended another five hundred feet. The mountainside looked like solid rock, and Jared worried the C-4 wouldn't be enough to do the job. "Let's do this thing that we like to do when we do things like this."

"Counting," Walt said. "Five, four, three, two, one."

A cloud of dust arose from the mountainside briefly before the muffled sound of the explosion reached Jared's ears, but the mountain remained intact. "Uh, we might have needed a bigger bomb."

Massive chunks of rock blasted from the mountainside, followed by a column of rolling black smoke. The sound wave from the explosion jolted the Intruder as it hovered.

"Whoa. That was badass," Jared said. "I think that first blast just lit the fuse. Thirty pounds of C-four can't pack that kind of punch."

After the dust and smoke cleared, Markus said, "I don't believe it. Half the mountain is gone."

The landing pad and the rest of the mountain underneath had vanished. The half that contained Element 115 remained intact. Then Jared felt lucky that blowing up the control panel didn't start a chain reaction that led to something akin to a nuclear explosion. They did not know what they were dealing with.

"Yeah," Hammer said. "Thirty pounds of C-four can't do that kind of damage. I only had enough C-four to obliterate the controls."

"I'll take that as a sign that the damage done will be enough to render the Stargate useless," Erik said.

"Can we go now?" Jared asked.

"You're the captain," Erik said.

"You got that right," Jared said. "Markus, get us out of here—*pronto*, as Gear would say."

"You need to work on your accent," Gear said.

"Work on this," Jared said with his hand outstretched and middle finger pointing to the sky.

The Intruder slowly moved away from the mountain and crossed the river. The camera zoomed in on the arena as the aircraft approached the coliseum.

"Hey, gladiators are getting ready to fight down there," Rat said. "Can we watch?"

"We don't need to see two men hacking away at each other," Jared said.

"Looks like there're three men," Gear said.

"They aren't fighting each other," Hammer said. "Two of them are protecting one on the ground."

"Yeah!" Rat said. "From a T. rex! Man, this is going to be awesome!"

"There's no way three men can defeat a Tyrannosaurus rex," Erik said. "Why, they only have swords as weapons."

"Blowing up the mountain may have bought them some time," Hammer said. "The crowd looks spooked."

"We can't let this happen," Markus said. "This is madness. Let's get them out of here."

"What about the Prime Directive?" Jared said. "Besides that, they might be criminals, and this is how they get punished."

"The three men in the arena are Russian soldiers. First Class Lieutenant Nikotay Pavlov, Third Lieutenant Mikhail Zaitsev, and Second Lieutenant Dmitriy Titov," Walt said.

"What? How do you know that?" Jared said.

"They, like you, have microchips implanted under the skin. We are close enough for me to read them," Walt said.

"Ruskies? That's going to make this fight even better!" Rat said.

There wasn't any time to argue. The T. rex would be on them in seconds. The crowd spotted the Intruder, and people pointed upward as they panicked.

"The Russians wouldn't be in this predicament if not for coming after us," Jared said. "Let's get them out of here."

The Intruder descended quickly and fired three rounds from the guns, dropping the T. rex to the ground.

The two Russians saw the aircraft and then looked at each other briefly before abandoning their swords and shields. They grabbed the one on the ground under his arms and waited for the Intruder to land.

Pandemonium swept throughout the coliseum as people pushed and shoved to leave.

The Intruder's landing gear touched the ground, and the loading door dropped. Jared stepped down and waved his hand, beckoning the soldiers to come.

The Russians didn't need any convincing and dragged their fallen comrade to the steps. Once there, they lifted the man to the reaching arms of the Intruder's crew, who pulled him to safety. The two soldiers quickly climbed the steps and into the Intruder.

Rat and Hammer had rifles pointing at the Russians, who stopped and raised their hands in front of their shoulders.

Jared said, "Even though you're dressed like Fred Flintstone and Barney Rubble, we know you are Russian soldiers."

The Russians glanced at each other but remained silent.

"And we know your names," Jared said. "Walt?"

"Pavlov, Zaitsev, and Titov," Walt said.

"Do you speak English?" Jared asked.

One soldier said, "I am Pavlov. We can speak English. They teach us the language of our enemy at a young age."

"Let's make this quick," Jared said. "Are there any more of you here?"

"One," Kolya Pavlov said.

"Where is he?" Jared asked. "We'll get him."

"He is in the belly of a dinosaur," Kolya said.

"Look, we just saved your ass. Don't make this any more difficult than it has to be," Jared said.

The unconscious man woke.

Gear took a knee by his side and examined him for wounds. "Do you know what's wrong with him?"

"He was exposed to a gas that rendered him unconscious," Kolya said. "He should be fine soon."

"We will attend to him now," Dima said.

"Bring him over there by the lockers," Hammer said. "Don't do anything you will regret. That is your only warning."

"Dima, you grab his feet, and I will get this end," Kolya said.

"No..." Misha said. "No. I can walk." The young man turned on his side and then on his knees. Kolya and Dima both helped him up.

"Pull down the jump seats and secure their arms and legs," Jared said.

Gear went next to the lockers and pulled down three jump seats. He retrieved a handful of yellow tie wraps and waited for the Russians to sit. Then, a tie wrap went around each pair of hands and set of legs at the ankles.

"We've done our good deed for the day," Jared said. "Markus, get us out of here."

The pilot waited for his teammates to sit, then lifted the Intruder off the ground and into the sky.

Time passed with Hammer sitting in his seat, turned toward the Russians, and rifle across his lap. The captives were calm and didn't complain or even ask for food or drink.

Jared couldn't help but wonder how the Russians found their way to the city or what they had suffered while captive. But it wasn't his job to interrogate the prisoners—at least, not this time. The team would be home soon enough, and Command would take control.

"We're approaching the exit point," Markus said. "Walt, you'll have to get us through. I'll be useless if our ride is anything like last time."

"Affirmative," Walt said.

The golf-ball-sized Element 115 started glowing and humming—a mist formed above the bismuth container. The box vibrated, but the spring clamps kept it from shimming off the table.

"Oh, I hate it when it does that," Jared said. "I don't want to toss my cookies."

The element's glow intensified, and Jared craned his neck to watch the mesmerizing glow. He floated on a sea of marshmallows as soft whispers passed over his ears. "Yes, Grandma...I hear you...Yes...There's no place like home...There's no place like home...There's no—"

Jared gasped as if he had just awoken at the top of a roller coaster, only to find it speeding down a four-hundred-foot drop. He took a second and felt his center of gravity return. "Walt, report."

"We are above the North Pole. Today is January ninth, Twenty Twenty-Five."

"We're back home, cuz!" Markus said.

The teammates hooped and hollered.

Erik threw a fist in the air and said, "*A-YEEE*! *Laissez les bons temps rouler*!"

"Setting course for Greenland," Markus said. "Three hours away."

Erik turned to Jared; his face masked by a troubled look. "The Russians. What will happen to them? They know we stole the element. If proof of that ever reached the Kremlin…it might become the spark that lights the powder keg."

"Well, Command will leave nothing to chance," Jared said. "You can bet on that."

"I understand," Erik said. "But it just seems so wrong…so unnecessary."

"If given the choice of three men dying instead of hundreds of millions…What would you choose?"

EPILOGUE

Lieutenant Ustinov sat in an uncomfortable folding metal chair behind a military field desk in the small room. Two file cabinets, with peeling paint and rusty, were to his left. Stacks of papers covered most of the desk, some strewn about haphazardly.

A knock on the door broke his reverie. "What?"

The door pushed open, and a soldier holding papers in one hand entered.

"Well?" Ustinov asked.

"Sir, three of our soldiers have arrived from the prisoner exchange with the Ukrainians," the soldier said.

"Give them a meal and send them back to the front," Ustinov said. "Like the rest of them."

"But, sir, there is an issue. These men are Special Forces not assigned to the Ukrainian conflict," the soldier said.

Ustinov lifted his eyes from his paperwork. "What are they doing here, then?"

Without an answer, the soldier handed the papers to Ustinov.

The lieutenant read the first page and then scanned the next two. "Bring them in. I want to hear their story."

"Yes, sir." The soldier stepped away briefly and brought the three men in before Ustinov.

He rose from his desk and looked at each man individually in the eye. "Pavlov, Titov, Zaitsev, where are the other men assigned to your team?"

Kolya kept his gaze straight ahead. Mechanically, he said, "We do not know their whereabouts."

"Where have you been?" Ustinov asked. "Look at you. Your skin—bronze from the sun. It is dead of winter."

"We woke in a Ukrainian prison camp five days ago and have no memory of how we were captured," Kolya said.

Ustinov ran his thumb and index finger across his lower lip. "What is your last memory?"

Looking back and forth at his comrades, Kolya said, "There was an explosion at a scientific laboratory outside of Moscow. Much damage was done. Many people died. We all remember learning of the event, but we can remember nothing beyond that."

"That incident happened over six months ago," Ustinov said.

Kolya said, "Then we have been traveling the last six months in darkness."

*

"Have a seat! Have a seat!" General Mitchell said as two men entered his office. "Congratulations on completing your mission—quite successfully, I might add. Element One-Fifteen will probably keep our scientists busy for the next decade. And the geneticists will have a field day with new medicines, food, and growing the prehistoric dinosaurs with the DNA collected."

"It was a team effort," Jared said as he sat. "Including Captain Lott."

"I was there to serve at your pleasure," Erik said after taking his seat.

Jared shot the Cajun a glance that called the biggest load of bullshit he'd ever heard.

"I was pleased we spared the lives of the three Russian soldiers," Erik said.

"Yes, well, you know modern technology," Mitchell said. "We're able to erase memories from the brain now. We could have even erased all their memories and reprogrammed them to be whoever we wanted, including spies in our service. But we didn't. The soldiers had been through so much that we gave them a pass."

Jared's face contorted. "General? Gave them a—OUCH!" He reached down and rubbed his left ankle.

Eric glanced at Jared and gave him a quick shake of the head. "I believe what Jared was going to say before having an unexpected cramp: Gave them a pass? My, how progressive we've become. How delightful in a strained world that we prove the United States of America operates for the good of all Mankind."

"Yes, well, here's a small token of my appreciation," General Mitchell said as he reached under his desk and pulled out two liquor bottles. "For you, Erik, a bottle of eighteen-year-old Laphroaig. Jared, Royal Crown Peach. My wife is a big fan of the peach flavor."

Jared and Erik thanked the general.

"Now, to address some questions you and your team brought up. We concluded that the objects found by the Neanderthal and ancient human camps were electronic fencing, as you suspected. Designed to keep the dinosaurs out. The fence by the river more than likely kept the Neanderthals and ancient humans from intermingling."

"Markus said the Neanderthal leader basically tried to tell him that," Jared said.

"You asked about your cologne. After some tests, it was determined that it was possible to act as an attractant—giving you a little more attention from the dinosaurs than you would have preferred," Mitchell said.

"Great," Jared said. "Just my luck."

"Moving on, learning of the Archeons was quite a surprise. The Stargate was the first actual evidence of extraterrestrial life, and it brought the possibility of traveling to other worlds. Unfortunately, you destroyed it without clearance from Command," General Mitchell said. "Some would have you reprimanded for such a hasty decision."

Jared raised a finger and opened his mouth, but Erik pulled his arm down and interrupted before the young man could speak. "The team agreed it was the best course, considering the seriousness of the threat. Knowing the Archeons could return any minute, we took advantage of the only opportunity we were sure to have."

"I understand," General Mitchell said. "So you know, I wasn't in the camp of those questioning your decision."

"We appreciate the commendations," Jared said. "My team and I look forward to our next assignment."

Erik leaned back in his chair and ran his bottom lip under his front teeth.

General Mitchell raised an eyebrow and asked, "Erik, you look troubled. Is there something on your mind?"

"Yes, General." He cleared his throat and leaned forward. "It's about the Archeons—The Watchers."

"Go on."

"From what I could gather from the text, the Archeons were a race who maintained a certain order in a sector of the Milky Way Galaxy. They travel through a Stargate that connects to many worlds. The issue is that one must build a Stargate on a planet before interstellar travel can occur. It's not The Watchers we have to be concerned with now. It's the Explorers who built the Stargate. What if they return?"

THE END

Check out other great

Dinosaur Thrillers!

Julian Michael Carver

TRIASSIC

After spending many years in artificial hypersleep, a handful of survivors of the exploration vessel Supernova awaken to find their ship torn to shreds. They are unsure of what happened in space or how they crashed into an uncharted planet. Upon exploration of the new world, they soon realize their destination: The Triassic, the first chapter of the Mesozoic Era. A plan is formulated to escape this terrifying landscape plagued with dinosaurs and prehistoric beasts. The survivors soon discover that there may be an even larger threat looming under the trees than just the dinosaurs, threatening to cut their mission short and trap them all forever in the primitive depths of the Triassic.

Hugo Navikov

THE FOUND WORLD

A powerful global cabal wants adventurer Brett Russell to retrieve a superweapon stolen by the scientist who built it. To entice him to travel underneath one of the most dangerous volcanoes on Earth to find the scientist, this shadowy organization will pay him the only thing he cares about: information that will allow him to avenge his family's murder. But before he can get paid, he and his team must enter an underground hellscape of killer plants, giant insects, terrifying dinosaurs, and an army of other predators never previously seen by man. At the end of this journey awaits a revelation that could alter the fate of mankind ... if they can make it back from this horrifying found world.

Check out other great

Dinosaur Thrillers!

Steve Metcalf

OBJEKT 221

Ruthless multi-national conglomerate Allied Genetics is under siege from a paramilitary force for hire. Allied calls in reinforcements and fortifies their crown-jewel property – an abandoned Soviet military facility in Crimea known during the Cold War as Objekt 221. Fortunately for the future of their research, O221 straddles a stretch of rocky landscape that hides a rift – a portal through time and space. Through this rift, Allied Genetics can travel, at will, to the Cretaceous – 100 million years into Earth's past – and bolster their genetic experiments with dinosaur DNA ... something their competitors want to stop at all costs."Objekt 221" is a story blending numerous science fiction elements such as repurposed military facilities, time travel, rogue corporate armies, dinosaurs and the hint of a super-ancient civilization.

Bestselling collection

PREHISTORIC:
A DINOSAUR ANTHOLOGY

PREHISTORIC is an action packed collection of stories featuring terrifying creatures that once ruled the Earth. Lost worlds where T-Rex and Velociraptors still roam and man is now on the menu. Laboratories at the forefront of cloning technology experiment with dinosaurs they do not understand or are able to contain. The deepest parts of the ocean where Megalodon, the largest and most ferocious predator to have ever existed is stalking new prey. Plus many more thrillers filled with extinct prehistoric monsters written by some of the best creature feature authors this side of the Jurassic period.

Check out other great

Dinosaur Thrillers!

P.K. Hawkins

THE LOST ISLAND

Scientists Dr. Eccleston and Dr. Lerner have done many routine expeditions for the Skurzon Corporation in the past, helping the company search the ocean for newly available resources freed by melting ice. They're expecting to maybe find oil at the bottom of the Arctic Sea. What they aren't expecting is a lost island that defies all scientific understanding. When something comes out of the sea and destroys their research vessel, the scientists and the rest of the crew are forced into a game of survival against forces no human being has ever seen alive. If they can survive the giant insect swarms, the man-eating plants, and the dinosaurs, they might be able to live to tell the tale. But when each passing moment reveals murderers in their midst, their survival starts to look less and less likely.

William Meikle

THE LAND BELOW

A treasure hunt into the deepest cave system in Europe takes a turn for the worst.Now rather than treasure it is survival that is at the forefront of the spelunkers' thoughts. But their attempt to escape out of the dark deep places is thwarted. Men are not at home in the depths. But there are things that are, pale terrifying things. Huge things.Things red in tooth and claw.

Printed in Dunstable, United Kingdom